Dale Mayer

TERK'S GUARDIANS
TREVOR 12

TREVOR: TERK'S GUARDIANS, BOOK 12
Beverly Dale Mayer
Valley Publishing Ltd.

ISBN-13: 978-1-778866-47-0
Print Edition

Books in This Series:

Radar, Book 1

Legend, Book 2

Bojan, Book 3

Langdon, Book 4

Walker, Book 5

Reid, Book 6

Sanders, Book 7

Nate, Book 8

Royal, Book 9

Alex, Book 10

Royce, Book 11

Trevor, Book 12

Morrison, Book 13

About This Book

Answering Terk's beacon, Trevor walks into the castle, not quite prepared to turn around and leave instantly for a job in Africa, but that's exactly what happened. Finding Reenie pulling into Bullard's compound right behind him, he is delighted to be there. She is a curly carrottop with a free spirit, whose looks alone set most people back. Then, when she spouts on about alarms and warnings of an electrical kind, … well, no wonder no one over is willing to listen.

Reenie hopes that people will take her seriously, but, so far, it hasn't worked out so well for her. However, finding Trevor at Bullard's just at the perfect time—to stand at her side and to validate her work—is both wonderful and awful that she needs that at all. Still, as the craziness unwinds around them, there's no one else she would rather with her.

Trevor and Reenie need to step up, as does each and every person in Bullard's compound. Everyone needs to be here 100 percent, as these attacks are, … let's say, … *very* personal.

Sign up to be notified of all Dale's releases here!

https://geni.us/DaleNews

PROLOGUE

TERKEL SAT IN the huge dining room, among several of his team. Terk, his arms full of babies, looked over at Celia.

She smiled as one of the twins stretched, smacking him on the cheek. "Kalen really likes your cheek," she murmured.

"Yeah, but it isn't Kalen. It's Daren," he murmured, as he kissed each baby on the top of their heads.

"Sounds like Royce completed yet another successful job, doesn't it?" she noted.

"Yes, he did a wonderful job on this one. Considering that he and Heather will both be here in a couple hours," he added, "I'm grateful we had a couple weeks in between jobs, so we caught a break on some things."

"Yes, it's nice to have at least some jobs that aren't so overtly dangerous. Some escorting and investigative work gives everyone a bit of a break on the stress element," she noted. "These ops that almost take my breath away are hard when I think that anybody could come close to getting killed. They are all our family, our growing family, and such a loss would just devastate everyone."

"Which is why we also won't go there," he reminded her. "That is not something we want to think about or to put out there in the ethers. We take all the precautions we can, but it's still our role in the world. I know it's hard, but it's a job that we must do because so few people are out there to do it."

"What about Riff?" she asked, looking back at the man currently collapsed on one of the big chairs in front of the fireplace.

"Riff's here," he called out. "I've been off doing my own stuff over the last couple months, but I'm still hoping you guys will come up with something to help me with my personal matter." He turned, glaring at Terkel.

"We may have a lead very soon," Terk replied in a clipped tone. "The gals are running it down, and, no, I'm not telling you until we know whether it's a good one or not."

Riff straightened up in the chair slowly. "It needs to happen soon."

Just then Angela walked in, looked at Riff, and snorted. "Of course you would be here."

"Yeah, I'm right here," he snapped, with a negligent shrug. "The question is, why are you here?"

"I came to do my usual check on the babies."

"*Right*," he muttered, getting to his feet. "I'll leave you to it then."

"You don't have to run away just because I'm here, you know?"

"Yes, I do," he declared, giving her a glare.

She shrugged. "Fine, if you're still running away, that's up to you. I thought maybe you'd grown up some."

He sucked in his breath, and everybody in the room sucked in theirs, waiting for an explosion. Riff slowly turned to face her, fire in his eyes. "What the hell does that mean?"

She stared at him, her hands going to her hips. "You know perfectly well what it means."

"No, I don't, and there's absolutely no point in talking to you until I have answers."

"The answers won't change the end result."

He stiffened, then nodded. "They won't change the end result, but they might change my attitude toward it."

"Ah, you better hurry it up then," she said, openly glaring now, "because I'm running out of patience." And, with that, she turned and walked out of the huge dining room. Riff exited via a doorway on the other side of the room.

Terkel glanced from Riff's back to Angela's back and then to Celia, who had a tiny smile tipping up the corners of her lips. Terk sighed. "We really do need to get answers for Riff."

"We do," she agreed, "but it'll be a while yet."

"I know, but hopefully not too long."

Just then Terk's phone rang. He checked the Caller ID and answered, "Hey, Bullard. How are you doing?"

"I'm okay, but I could use some help."

"You've got it. What do you need?"

"Somebody's hacking into my system."

"You don't need our help for that," Terk noted. "Your team is better on that IT sort of thing than we are."

"Yeah, except this is energy-related," he snapped. "I don't know what they're doing or how they're doing it, but they're attacking my system with energy."

"Energy?" Terk repeated.

"Yeah, somebody keeps shutting everything down."

"You might need to consider that it's not energy."

"I would, except for somebody named Tangerine—and who the hell names their kid after an orange? Anyway, Tangerine, who calls herself Reeni, or whatever the hell she said," he muttered in disgust, "she came to my damn front door and announced that we needed help and that she was here to help us."

"You don't believe her?" Terk asked.

"Everything she's talking about makes life even more of a mockery," he admitted. "How do you listen to somebody named Tangerine in the first place?"

"Listen to her," Terkel ordered, "because she means it."

Bullard stopped, pausing before he spoke again. "Don't tell me that she's one of yours."

"She's not one of mine, and I don't know her. However, I can check her energy from right here, and she's got a lot of power," he shared. "More so, she's utilizing it to the benefit of others' good—to your good. So that's a very interesting combination."

"Great, but I don't trust her. I won't work with her if I don't have somebody from your team or at least somebody who's vetted Tangerine to say that she's on the up-and-up."

"Interesting, and you also need help solving who's after your system?"

"Of course I do," he snapped once more. "At least if you come and confirm what she's saying, then we'll have a better idea about what's going on—preferably before I lose all communications again. Pretty sure we've got hacking going on. I just don't know at what level and by whom, so send somebody and fast." With that, Bullard, as grumpy as ever, ended the call.

Terk looked around at everybody else seated at the big dining room table. "Do we have anybody? Most are off or at least committed to jobs here and there right now, aren't they?"

"We have a couple potentially available team members," Celia replied, "and we also have a bunch of applications for new hires. We just haven't had a chance to assess them."

"Yeah, well, they are hardly applications when they're sent in on the ethers," Terk pointed out, with a note of humor.

"Hey," Celia countered, rounding on him instantly, "you sent out a beacon, saying that you had work, so don't be surprised when people respond in kind."

"I should never have done that," he muttered. "It brought in too many weirdos."

"They're all weirdos one way or another, and you know that."

"I know. I know. I know. I keep saying that it doesn't matter, but some of these people are very *unique*," he replied.

"And we need somebody unique right now," Celia stated, "somebody who can go into Bullard's place, handle all of it, and deal with whatever is going on in his world. We owe Bullard, and he's a friend, so we'll obviously help him."

"We'll definitely help him," Terk confirmed.

Just then everybody heard the front door opening. They all checked the energy, found friendlies approaching, and waited to see who had arrived. When Wade walked in, he smiled at everybody and pointed behind him. "Hey, guess who I found outside?"

TREVOR STEPPED FORWARD, a big grin on his face.

"Look who's here. It's the big man himself." Terkel hopped up, handed off the babies to Celia, and walked over to give this old friend a big hug. "Good God," he muttered, as he stared at Trevor. "I haven't heard from you in forever."

"Not until you sent out a damn beacon. What are you, nuts?"

"Yeah, I was discussing that just now with my wife."

At that term, Trevor's eyebrows popped up. "Wife?" He looked at the woman holding two babies and frowned. "Kids too?"

"Yeah," Terk stated proudly.

"So, you got soft in your old age or what?"

"I didn't think so, but that beacon idea wasn't my best," he admitted.

"On the other hand, it brought me in," Trevor said cheerfully. "So what kind of work have you got?"

"You ever been to Africa?" Gage asked from the sidelines, as he got up and walked over to shake hands.

"Yeah, but not for a few years though. That's where Bullard is."

"You know Bullard?" Gage asked.

"I do, although I'm not sure that he particularly likes my style. I'm a little too unrestrained for him."

"Oh, he's also mellowed quite a bit," Celia added, with a smile. "He's married with kids as well."

"Wow, the shocks just don't quit," Trevor murmured, still staring at the woman holding twins.

She got up, walked over, and introduced herself. "I'm Celia, and Terkel is my husband."

Her hands held two babies, so he didn't bother shaking her hand. "Pleased to meet you." He turned to Terkel and said, "Lucky guy, you. How did that happen?"

Terkel snorted. "Don't ask, but you're damn right, and I know it. Still, I do have a job right now that needs somebody to turn around and head to Bullard's place."

"I'm on it," Trevor replied. "Do I get to find out what the job is now or later?"

Sophia came in and replied, "Later. Here's your file with

all the information, but you need to get to the airport fast."

Trevor checked his watch, grabbed the file, then lifted a hand and waved. "We'll talk later, after this job." And, with that, Trevor was gone.

CHAPTER 1

TREVOR ACKERS DEPLANED at the airport and hopped into his rental truck and headed out toward Bullard's place. He didn't know if anybody had warned Bullard that Trevor was coming, but he hoped so. It was all about preparation in their industry, and certainly some things one needed to be prepared for.

Now, Tangerine, on the other hand, was somebody nobody could really be prepared for. He'd met her in the past. She was a free spirit who came from a very wealthy family of citrus growers, hence her name. Her personality and her work mode and her abilities were all very unconventional. Regardless, she was definitely out there to help people. Still, most people didn't take well to her free-energy-wielding spirit.

Trevor couldn't imagine the taciturn Bullard handling her at all, particularly if she'd just shown up unannounced at his door, which was what apparently happened. Showing up without any warning didn't sound like a good approach at all when working with Bullard. For his part, Trevor was looking forward to seeing her again—Bullard too, for that matter. Tangerine and Bullard would definitely get on each others' nerves, simply because they were both fairly dominant. Although, according to Terk, things had calmed somewhat, now that Bullard was married with kids himself.

That blew away Trevor. To even see the progress these men had made in their personal lives was something Trevor wasn't accustomed to. He should have been, though. He knew an awful lot of people in the industry and had certainly noted the movement toward stable relationships and having kids. That included people he didn't think would ever go in that direction, like Levi.

And now almost everybody who worked for Levi was married with children too. Trevor felt old all of a sudden, questioning where he was going and why he'd been so determined to not go into that deeper level with someone and to have a special relationship on a permanent basis. That was a whole different story, completely different than a hook-up or the short-term relationships that were a great—but temporary—break from the realities of life.

Trevor drove toward Bullard's compound, knowing he still had a couple hours on the road, but he already felt something shifting inside him. Sensing something dead wrong, he put his pedal to the metal to speed up. He didn't have the same talents that a lot of Terk's team did. Trevor received more of a global suspicion of things that were wrong in the world, and he now definitely got a lot of negative energy coming from the direction of Bullard's place.

It more than came from that direction. It had been very specifically parked there, as in he could tell that something was very wrong. Tangerine had been right. Tangerine was never wrong. The problem was that she wasn't terribly subtle in the way that she let people know. She figured everybody should automatically believe her, even though nobody had a clue who she was. Plus, she presented herself in such an odd way that a lot of people more or less mocked her instead of listening to her warnings.

Not only were her mannerisms that of a free spirit, but her tight carrot-top of curls were distracting. The last time he'd seen her, her hair had been a little past her shoulders. Yet she had that air about her that was all business, all science, all data. Still, at first glance, people just couldn't quite handle her eccentricities. She was very much the opposite of the conventional business types, the nerdy scientists, and certainly the data-driven accountants. Trevor grinned in anticipation, knowing that he would see her again.

According to what he'd been told, Bullard hadn't let her into the compound, but she was staying close by until somebody else arrived to verify her. That it would be Trevor was a bonus and added to his anticipation. Those were the thoughts that occupied his mind as he raced to his destination.

Eventually, as he pulled into the main driveway to the compound and waited for somebody to respond on the security intercom at the gate, he couldn't stop grinning as a vehicle pulled in right behind him.

The driver looked very much to be Tangerine. She drove a white SUV and appeared to be alone. He quickly spoke into the security box, and the gate opened. He drove in, and she came in right behind him without any hesitation. So either she was expected or … she did one of her energy tricks. At least that's the way he saw it. Things like electronic gates, she could open regardless of what security lock was on them. Trevor was a little surprised that she had let that gate stand between her and Bullard. Trevor also didn't think she had the patience to wait almost a day for him to show up. Maybe she had mellowed too? He doubted it.

Trevor pondered all that, also wondering if Tangerine's

gifts or abilities had clued her into Bullard's predicament. Trevor would ask her about it sooner rather than later. He pulled up in front of the compound and hopped out. Several men stepped outside. Trevor grinned as he recognized a bunch of them, even Dave, somebody he hadn't seen in a long time. Multiple handshakes and bro-hugs ensued. Then he watched as everybody fell silent. At that point, he knew Tangerine was here. He turned to face her. "Hey, Reeni."

She stared at him, and her face lit up as she threw herself into his arms. He gave a big laugh and hugged her close. "I forgot how exuberant you were."

"How could you forget?" she asked, frowning at him, as she quickly hugged him again. "Not to mention the fact that it's so nice to see a welcoming face," she whispered.

He chuckled and turned to the others to see astonishment and a sense of relief in their expressions, since he'd obviously recognized Reeni. He smiled at Bullard, who'd just arrived too, and reached out to shake his hand. "Hey, long time no see."

Bullard eschewed the handshake and wrapped an arm around him. "So glad you could come. It's been a while."

"I hear lots of changes are afoot." Trevor grinned. "You could have blown me away when I found out Terk had twins."

"Not just Terk, but several others on his team had twins too." Bullard shook his head. "Something to do with all that energy confined in one place."

At that, Trevor contemplated it for a moment, then nodded. "You could be right about that. I hadn't considered the side effects."

"Oh, I don't think they did either, … until it was too late." He gave Trevor a sly grin. "I know they're all trying to figure it out before round two gets underway, but everybody, absolutely everybody from his original team, has wives and family now. And all of them were pregnant within the same few months."

Trevor laughed and laughed. "That is amazing and seems very appropriate."

Wrapping his arm around Tangerine's shoulders again, Trevor looked at the gang and announced, "I see you guys have already met Reeni."

Curiosity filled most of their expressions, and some remained reserved. Nervous laughter came from some, as several of the men nodded.

Trevor smiled. "Reeni and I certainly aren't strangers," he admitted. "We've worked together on a couple research projects."

"And they were fun," Reeni interrupted, beaming at everybody. "You guys are so lucky to have him. If I'd known he was coming to handle this, I wouldn't have stepped in."

He looked at her and grinned. "Are you kidding? Stepping in is what you do best, particularly when nobody's expecting you *and* you're not invited."

She rolled her eyes at that. "You make me sound as if I'm always in the way and bursting into places where I don't belong."

He belted out a laugh. "Lots of times you are," he declared. "On the other hand, you're all heart, and that's important." At that comment, he gave Bullard a very pointed look.

Bullard nodded, a smile on his face, his shoulders relaxed. "In that case, we do need to do a little bit of work because I don't know what the hell's going on."

Trevor asked Tangerine, "Did you find a source for this problem?"

She shook her head. "No, I could tell it was coming from here but not necessarily how or why. The source of the problem is still here," she noted, looking at each of the men gathered out front. "In the time that I've been here, I haven't found the culprit."

"Everybody here doesn't want a culprit found among them," Trevor pointed out to her.

"Yeah," she muttered, with an eyeroll, "but life doesn't work that way."

Such a note of age-old weariness filled her tone that Trevor frowned at her.

She gave him a small smile. "Let's just say that life hasn't been all that easy for me over these last few years."

He hated to hear that because one of the things he'd always admired about her was her consistently upbeat attitude. "Surely you didn't let life beat you down, did you?" he asked.

"No, sometimes family just likes to beat you down."

He winced. Family was one thing he did know she had trouble with. Her family had a big, important, well-known name, and she was, well, he didn't want to say an embarrassment to them, but, yeah, an embarrassment to them. "Still razzing you, *huh*?" he asked.

"They'll never understand me," she declared, facing him.

"No, they won't, and, as I told you the last time, you need to accept that they won't change, then just do what you need to do."

She didn't say anything to that. She turned to the others and beamed. "Any chance I could get some coffee?"

Dave laughed. "Absolutely. We're just waiting for *the okay* from the boss."

She squared her shoulders and faced Bullard. "You're the boss. Is that an okay or a no?"

"It's an okay," he replied, staring at her with mild curiosity. "You really do that energy stuff too, *huh*?"

She shrugged. "I'm not sure I do anything, though apparently that's what my family considers to be my eccentricities," she replied, with a note of asperity in her voice. "But, if you listen to Trev here, you'll find out I can do quite a bit. It's all electrical stuff. But the rest? ... Well, I don't understand the rest of it."

"And yet it's all related," Trevor added. "One thing I never quite understood is how you could only deal with electrical signals, when energy is energy."

"Says you. You're the one who floats up to the bloody sky and looks down on top of the world to see where there's trouble." She stared at him. "How can you possibly say you don't understand, when I'm only stuck on electrical energy?"

He grinned. "Okay, touché on that one."

She glanced at the others, rolled her eyes, and laughed. "We're attracting attention," she muttered to Trevor.

"No, that would be you," he clarified, with a grin. "You're very good at that part."

She glared at him. "I am not, and I don't do it on purpose. So," she warned, "don't you even go there."

"Of course not," he said. "That orange hair and that love-of-life attitude, there's really no going anywhere with that. You're a free spirit, always have been, so you just need to accept it and go on."

"I have," she declared, poking his chest for emphasis. "It's other people who have a problem with it."

He smiled, looked over at the group of men staring at the two of them in fascination, then told her in an audible whisper, "Don't look now, but I think we're drawing a crowd."

She sighed. "I should be used to it, *huh?*"

"You should be, but you aren't, so that's no different," he noted cheerfully, then motioned at the door. "Shall we go in?"

At that, the group all moved back, and Trevor nudged her forward. She stopped in the entranceway, took a big deep breath of energy, and sighed. "Clearly a lot of love is in this place."

"There is," Bullard agreed, studying her intently. "And we want to keep it that way."

CHAPTER 2

REENI STARED AT Bullard and nodded. "Not sure if a warning is in that comment or not, but I have no intention of disrupting your family life in any way," she murmured. "I honestly came to help."

"If that's the case," he said, "then you're more than welcome. But the business that we work in, that we live in, … it's not always full of people willing to help, particularly for nothing."

"Right, and that's the world I was trying to get away from, but it's not that easy. It seems as if it's everywhere."

"It is," he agreed, still studying her.

Even now she felt his gaze intently on her face, and then it shifted to Trevor. The fact that Trevor was here thrilled her to no end. She'd always loved the guy. He was special in so many ways, and a lot of it was the fact that he accepted her for who she was. It was hard to get that acceptance from anybody else, and it was definitely something she recognized in him.

As she was led into a very large kitchen and through to a dining area, she stopped at the threshold and frowned. "There has been violence in here."

Trevor, staying at her side, wrapped an arm around her. "I gather it's not just electrical anymore."

"It is, and yet it isn't," she muttered in a bewildered

tone. "It's starting to get more emotional, and I don't like it," she announced in resignation.

He chuckled. "No, I can't imagine you would. Yet you run on a lot of emotions yourself."

"Maybe that's why I recognize it now."

"You'll have to fill me in on what happened," Trevor stated, "because, if your abilities have changed, that's a big one."

"I don't know that they've changed, … just grown maybe. Yet"—she held up a hand—"it is connected to electrical energy around me. I just can't really explain it."

"You don't have to, certainly not to me." Trevor gave her a reassuring smile.

She smiled back at him. "I remember that too. You were always really good at acceptance."

"I would hope so, since it's essential in the field we're in, whether we choose to be in it right now or not. It is very much about acceptance. You and I both know that, just as soon as you think you know something, something happens, and you feel as if you don't know anything at all."

"Yes," she murmured, "that's very true."

She sensed his intense gaze, but she ignored it. She would have to explain it all to him at some point in time, but not when everybody else was here, practically breathing down their necks. They didn't know who she was before, so they wouldn't understand the changes, or what had brought them on anyway. Plus … it was personal. Personal, private, and not something she really wanted to advertise. She also knew that Trevor wouldn't mind in the least.

Bullard admitted, "Now that I understand you do all this energy work, you and I won't be butting heads so much."

Trevor laughed behind her. "I wasn't about to tell you either," he shared. "If I'd known you had any dealings with Terk, then maybe, but otherwise no way would I let anybody know. The fact that you do deal with Terk means I can talk about it because you have some understanding of what goes on."

At that, Bullard shook his head. "No way anybody can understand that shit," he declared, staring at him. "That's just too far beyond, and to think that this woman, … Reeni here, walked right up to my front door to tell me that I had a saboteur in my electrical field—at a time when we were already having a ton of electrical problems—it just pushed me past my limit."

"That makes sense," Trevor agreed, chuckling.

Reeni listened to the others, but, as their voices lowered, she couldn't hear anymore. She figured they had decided that she was not a fraud and was only here to help. At least she hoped that's what they were sharing among themselves. So, ignoring their mutterings, she stepped inside the dining room.

Dave smiled at her and pointed. "Coffee is on the sideboard."

She headed there, where another woman joined her. Reeni smiled at the incredibly happy woman and introduced herself. "Hi, I'm Reeni."

"I'm Leia, Bullard's wife. Or he's my husband rather." She laughed. "It's all a matter of perspective."

"It is, indeed." Reeni studied the woman with interest. "This is quite the place you've got here."

"It is. It's really great. I've been incredibly happy here, although I suspect that the purpose of your visit won't be one I like."

At that, Reeni winced. "I'm sorry. I hate to be the bearer of bad news, but it's much better to deal with a problem as soon as it pops up than let it develop into something that's much harder to deal with."

"I agree with you totally," Leia stated. "Absolutely I do. If you can help with this, please do. I don't want anything to mar the perfect family life I've built up here." Then she laughed nervously. "Though I know that sounds foolish because we can't protect and control everything."

"No, but you can do a lot when it comes to protecting things in life," Reeni shared. She loved Leia's energy, so calm and peaceful, and yet a sense of having already been to hell and back was there too—at least once, if not more. "If you have already had some bad incidents in life, the motivation to do what you need to do is that much higher."

"Absolutely," Leia agreed. "I feel as if I've already been through a lot, and I don't want anything else to go wrong, not again."

"Of course not," Reeni replied.

"We've certainly had a few other incidents and exposures to people who do energy work," Leia noted, "and I've been blessed to have one help me through childbirth."

"That's absolutely wonderful," Reeni murmured. "The healers do such an incredible job, and, all too often, miracles are the result—literally."

"I won't argue with that." She gave Reeni a bright smile, as she handed her a cup of coffee. She asked politely, "You take anything in it?"

Reeni shook her head. "No, I don't, thank you." As she accepted it, a buzz filled the air, and the lights flickered. She frowned, handing the coffee back to Leia. "Hang on to that for a minute." With that, she headed to where Trevor was.

He looked at her and nodded. "Yes, I feel it."

She smiled. "I forgot how much of a ground you were."

"Not just a ground but an accelerator too," he added, with a laugh.

"So, it's not just the bird's-eye view thing," she teased.

He nodded. "Definitely not."

At that, Bullard stepped in and asked curiously, "Hey, what's going on?"

Trevor looked over at him. "No attack is happening yet, … but a definite buzz of energy is here right now," he explained. "That's causing your lights to flicker."

The men gathered around, one of them asking, "When you say, *not an attack*, what do you mean?"

Nodding, Trevor replied, "Not an attack *this time*." Then he faced Reeni. "I definitely get the feeling that the intruder is testing the limits."

She nodded. "That makes sense, though I don't deal in the world where people would want to be testing such things. Unfortunately, now that you mention it, I see that as a possible option."

"It is, no doubt about it," Trevor declared. "That's what I'm getting right now." He walked closer to Bullard and gave him a wry look. "We need a list of anybody who you think might want to attack you these days. I know it'll be a substantial list, but I don't see any other way to do this. Also do you know anybody who does energy work who would hate you?"

Bullard stared at him. "I don't know anybody who does energy work, outside of Terk and his team, and I know Terk and his people wouldn't do this. So, what you're really asking me for is an all-encompassing enemies list. … Jesus, are there really so many of you guys, *Terk*'s guys?" Bullard looked confused as hell.

Trevor nodded and motioned Reeni over.

She joined them and added, "It really is somebody who knows you, but it could just as well be money related. I don't know what your financial situation is, but an awful lot of attacks lately were where people utilized energy to steal."

He stared at her expectantly. "Steal what?"

She shrugged. "Banking information for one, identities for another. That isn't what I would expect in this situation, but I don't really have any knowledge of what *this* is yet. All I can tell you is that, whatever you're keeping under wraps here, it is valuable, and somebody wants it."

At that came hard muttering from the group around them, and she took a step back, knowing that she had delivered bad news. Still, they were better off knowing than not knowing. She couldn't stop the warm sense of companionship she felt when Trevor wrapped an arm around her shoulders.

He leaned into her and whispered, "It's all right, you know?"

"Is it?" she murmured. "They don't know me, and they had to bring you along in order to even listen to what I had to say."

He laughed. "Think about what you're saying and about the group of men gathered here you're saying this to. They're all about following evidence and having proof, something they can see. Bullard's team might know Terk, but they don't know you. Terk heads up a large group of people like us now, so the word is getting around. Yet you're an unknown element. Whether you were associated with Terk's group or not, chances are you would still be treated the same."

She gave a headshake. "Talk about suspicious."

He burst out chuckling. "That's what they do, and being suspicious has kept them safe all this time," he explained. "So don't judge them for that. Now all we can do is help them adjust by giving them some tangibles that they can work with."

"Tangibles would be excellent," Bullard confirmed, frowning at him. "Have you got something concrete instead of this potentially nefarious somebody-wants-what-I-have idea?"

"You already know that somebody wants what you have," Trevor stated, locking gazes with him. "You have money. You have this compound, three to date that I know of. You have a team with impressive skills. You have a medical team as well. You have a family. You have even more than that. In fact, you have lots of things that people want." At Bullard's confused look, Trevor continued. "I'm not necessarily talking specifics, but consider somebody who hates you, consider somebody who may have just recently checked in out of the blue and realized, instead of suffering, you're doing incredibly well."

At that, Bullard glared at him. "So, you're saying this is personal."

"To attack your home, the home of your friends, your wife and theirs, plus the children?" Trevor slowly nodded. "It's a hell of a lot more than personal."

At that, all the other men agreed. "So, we need to take this on as a mission," suggested one of the men close by, "and we need to get to the bottom of it quickly."

Trevor agreed, and Reeni watched as they basically made decisions and didn't even bring her into it. It was such a weird feeling knowing that she's the one who started this ball rolling, but, until Trevor arrived, nobody was willing to even listen to her. She sighed.

He chuckled and pulled her closer. "It's not because you're female or a redhead or anything else. Believe me on that, because too many strong women are around here for these men to get away with that. This is just because you're an unknown factor."

"Yeah, I heard that the first time you mentioned it."

One of the men looked at her and nodded. "Even now, it's not that we don't believe you, but again we don't know you. We do have some experience with Trevor, and, of course, we all know Terk."

She nodded. "So, if I were part of Terk's team, would you trust me?"

"A lot more," he replied cheerfully, as he walked over to grab a cup of coffee. "A whole lot more."

TREVOR WATCHED REENI'S disgruntled expression take over her demeanor and smiled at her. "Good reason to affiliate yourself with Terk, you know?" he muttered in a low voice.

She shrugged. "I've never met him, so I haven't exactly been welcomed into his inner circle."

"It's not as if there was an inner circle, or any inner circle that existed. Up until maybe a year ago, nobody was really being invited in," he shared, with a chuckle. "After his world blew up, quite literally, things have changed. He's now gone private—not only just private, but also he's got a bigger team than ever who does this work."

She stared at him, fascinated. "You mean it when you

say *this work*, don't you?"

"I absolutely do," he confirmed. "I'm not necessarily such a big part of the energy work, but, when Terk sent out a call, I couldn't resist coming and checking out what he had going on."

"Is he the one who sent out that beacon?" she asked, puzzled. "I heard it, but I didn't really know who was calling, or even know what for."

"Oh, that was Terk all right," Trevor declared, with a wry smile. "I think he may regret it now. However, he was desperate to see how many other people were on the ethers."

"Too many," she muttered.

At that, Trevor burst out laughing. "You and I might say too many, but, when you're looking for more people like us, we can never have too many."

She shrugged. "Still, it seems to be a foolish thing to do."

"I think Terk's thinking the same thing, but it did bring me to him, although I've known him and many of his team members for years."

"That's the thing. You already know him. You already have a relationship with him," she pointed out. "I don't, and I doubt that he would want anything from me."

Trevor eyed her, puzzled. "More to the point, what do you have to offer the team, in terms of going out and helping the world? That's what would interest Terk."

"He really is into helping the world, *huh*?"

"He absolutely is," Trevor declared. "That was the main thing I was thinking of when I made the suggestion that you should affiliate yourself with him. He also has a lot of women on his team now." He watched her eyebrows shoot up, and he chuckled. "Remember, no judgment."

"Sure, no judgment, but that's still easier said than done."

"Absolutely," he agreed. "Yet Terk is not somebody you can ever pigeonhole into a particular box. He works on a lot of different premises, and he's quite open to many different types of people. So just keep that in mind, while you figure this out."

She nodded and didn't say anything more, and he appreciated that. She'd had enough judgments against her over the years, but he knew that an association with Terk was something completely different. So, if she could get her mind wrapped around it, she would be better off. He already thought it would be a good idea for her to be associated with Terk, but that wouldn't happen until Terk saw what she could do, how she did it, and how she conducted herself out in the world, all because there was no shortage of ways to get yourself killed.

Terk would never want that to happen in his name. Even as Trevor considered that, a banging came on the front door, and he watched as Damon soon strode in. Instantly came shouts and greetings as people gathered to greet him, and Damon smiled broadly. Trevor watched as his friend came over and smacked him on the shoulder.

"Have you got this solved yet?" Damon asked, with a big grin. When he caught sight of Reeni, his gaze widened, and the smile fell off his face.

Trevor thought it was almost a comical reaction to Reeni. She did make an entrance, just by standing there.

She nodded at Damon. "I'm Tangerine, but everyone can call me Reeni."

He nodded. "I should have guessed," he noted, with a bright chuckle. "I was told you had bright red hair."

"What you mean is orange hair, just like my namesake." She sighed. "I was born with this hair, and that's why my father decided I should carry this ridiculous moniker."

"I'm glad he had a sense of humor," Damon replied. "Not sure it's the easiest name to go through life with, though."

"Nope, it wasn't," she agreed, studying him, "but then neither is yours."

His eyebrows shot up. "I don't remember giving you mine."

"You're Damon, one of Terk's right-hand men."

"That's true enough," he stated, looking at her, "but we really are all part of the same team. We consider ourselves part of Bullard's team too."

"How does that work?" she asked. "There's always one boss."

"There can be one boss and a lot of second bosses," he said, with a smile. "When you're part of a team, small or large, you always have somebody who is ultimately responsible for major decisions. However, when you're in a team with Terk, he lets you have a lot of input into how you want things to be."

Reeni listened, while reading his aura. He seemed completely calm and collected.

Damon continued. "So, we don't look at it so much as Terk's rule, but as a compilation of all our wishes," he explained, with a smile.

"That works for you?" she asked.

"It absolutely does, and it's hard to imagine working with anybody else. We almost shut down shop here a while ago. If not for outside forces taking an even uglier turn in our world, we might have and would have all gone our own separate ways. That would have been a terrible shame because what we can do now, what we've accomplished, it's massive."

She smiled. "That's how it's supposed to be. Together you're supposed to do so much more than when you're apart. That's what relationships are all about too," she said, her tone gentle.

"I would agree with that as well." He reached out a hand and said, "Nice to meet you, Reeni."

She chuckled. "Same." Then she looked back at Trevor. "I suppose Trevor told you all about me."

"Not really. He told us a little bit but not a whole lot. He just mentioned that you were very unique."

She snorted. "Yeah, if that's all he told you, he was being kind." Everyone looked at her. She shrugged. "I've had an awful lot of names thrown at me, and, truth be told, to my family I'm a complete embarrassment, and they want me to take a long walk off a short pier. At this point in my life, I just have to ignore them, but that doesn't make it any easier."

"Some families are that way," Trevor agreed, "yours especially. They expected you to grow up and either be a trophy wife or arm candy," he shared, knowing she was not a fan of the topic. "You never had to work for a living, and so doing what you're doing just adds to your family's ire."

"Right. They think I'm some charlatan out here, making life crazy for people," she muttered. "They don't understand that it's a calling, something I have to do. I'm compelled to help, whether I want to or not."

"Lots of people don't understand the work we do," Damon chimed in, eyeing her carefully. "It's a matter of understanding and learning about energy and what energy does. And, more so, what it is that you can do for others while using your energy gifts."

"I'm still learning about my gifts," she admitted, "and

sometimes it comes more easily than other times."

"That is part and parcel of the work we do," Damon noted. "If you were to hook up with somebody a little more adept than yourself, you would find that your skills would grow in leaps and bounds. In our group alone, our skills have changed on a proportionate level that none of us could ever have anticipated."

At that, she stared at him in wonder. "Really?"

"Absolutely," he declared. "New abilities appear every day that we hadn't seen or recognized as being in the realm of possibilities, but now, for us, … it's commonplace."

"And you?"

"What about me?" Damon asked, with a smile.

"What is your gift?" she asked.

"I work as a ground, but I also manipulate energy. However, I certainly don't manipulate electronics." He turned to Bullard. "Have you picked up any tricks while I wasn't looking?"

Bullard snorted. "If I did, you can bet it wouldn't be to hack my own system."

"Maybe not, but did you piss off anybody lately?"

Bullard winced. "I wouldn't have thought so, but, as you well know, in our line of work, it could be anybody."

"Did you fire anybody recently?" Damon asked.

Bullard frowned at that, looked over at his team, and they all slowly shook their heads.

Damon nodded. "Okay. Have you had any arguments with suppliers, any of your old contractors? Has anybody threatened you, anything along that line?"

Trevor watched in amusement as Damon, knowing Bullard better than Trevor did, poked and prodded, forcing Bullard to contemplate these angles, to think about where they were at, who they might have pissed off, and what might be going on in their world. Bullard would be a little defensive when dealing with these issues. Yet everybody seemed to think about it and tossed questions around a couple times, not really landing on a suspect.

Trevor looked over at Reeni and found her staring at one of the rooms off to the side. "What's the matter?" he asked.

She shrugged and then nodded her head toward the room. "That room, it's wrong."

Bullard stared at her in exasperation. "What do you mean, it's *wrong*?" he asked in a confused tone. "How can it be wrong? It's just a room."

She glared at Bullard, and Trevor could see part of the reason why people got upset with her. She was right in the sense that, if she was picking up something, chances were, something could very well be wrong with that room. However, by saying *it was wrong* didn't tell anybody anything useful. Trevor asked her, "Can you give us any more details than that?"

"I need to go in there," she stated boldly, "but it's not my house, and I haven't been invited." With that, she stared at Bullard in anticipation.

Bullard frowned at her, still unsure of her antics.

Damon motioned for her to move. "Let's take a walk." Without listening to any arguments one way or another—or waiting for Bullard's permission—Damon led her directly into the room that bothered her.

Immediately Trevor came up behind them and noted it was a server room. "This would definitely be a room you would pick up on. That's for sure," Trevor said, right beside her.

She nodded and pointed to one of the big server banks.

"There's a problem with *that*."

Bullard groaned. "Yeah, well, hang on a minute. Are you a hacker? Do you understand computer systems?" Bullard asked from behind her.

She shook her head. "No, I'm not, and, no, I don't," she snapped, turning to look at him. "I get it. You don't want to listen to anything I have to say, but at least these two guys won't discount my words."

"And that's good," Bullard muttered, as he shook his head. "Then I don't have to worry about it."

She wasn't sure exactly what Bullard meant, but it's obvious he thought it was self-explanatory. She sighed and looked at Trevor. "So, this is where it gets problematic."

"The problem," Trevor began, "is that you need to give these guys more information. You say there's something wrong with the server bank, but are you saying that somebody has hacked into it?"

At that question, several of Bullard's men stiffened.

Trevor continued with his questions to prod more information from Reeni. "Are you saying that somebody has manipulated the hardware here, meaning, gotten in and sabotaged the hardware, or is it more about the software? What is it that you're saying exactly? Just go with your gut."

She frowned at him and looked back at the others. "Oh, sorry. I just figured they would know, once I pointed it out."

"No, they won't know," Trevor stated. "What do you see? What's the problem? Is the energy sparking the problem?"

She walked over and placed her hand on one of the servers.

"That bank is the problem?" he asked. "Or one of the actual disks?"

She tapped a single disk. "This one, this is causing the trouble."

Immediately one man walked over, one of Bullard's team, but Trevor wasn't sure he'd met him before.

Bullard stared at her. "That part of the server controls the satellite." He was more or less talking to himself.

She stared at him, her eyes huge. "You guys have a satellite? Your own satellite?"

Trevor laughed. "That's the thing," he explained to Bullard and Damon. "She doesn't know very much about electronics in the sense of how to hack or how to use any of this stuff. However, she can see the energy. She can recognize where the problem is, and she may even be able to trace it somewhat. Yet she doesn't know that you have a satellite. She doesn't know anything about your world. And remember that she came here to help. Before you go to all-out war, let's give her a chance to help."

"I'm all for that," Damon muttered, as he looked at Bullard sideways and gave him a nod. "She's right. The energy on this particular disk is, … I'll say, *off*."

"Okay, so that's not helping me either," Bullard grumbled in frustration. "What does *off* mean?"

Damon burst out laughing. "Other energy is on this disk, energy that's not yours. It looks nothing like your energy or like the energy of anybody else here. Now, the question is, have you had any work done by an outside contractor?"

Immediately everybody shook their heads.

Bullard frowned at Damon. "No, we handle all our own systems work here ourselves. You know that." Bullard stared at the piece of equipment they pointed to distrustfully. "So, are you saying it's been hacked, and I've got somebody in this system, like right now?"

She replied, "It's been hacked but ..." She looked over at Trevor.

Trevor nodded. "Even if it's crazy, spit it out, and we'll try to decipher it as best we can." He raised an eyebrow at Damon, adding, "We'll try anyway."

She shrugged. "Ghosties are in it."

At that, silence fell.

CHAPTER 3

REENI GLARED AT Trevor, who struggled to hold in his laughter, even as snorts of disgust erupted from the others.

"When you say, *ghosties*," Trevor began, "what does that mean to you?"

"It means foreign energy is there, almost as if from somebody who's not here. … I feel energy that doesn't belong to anybody else here. I feel energy that's come from a distance, as if it traveled here." She spoke in bits and pieces, then, embarrassed, she dropped her head. "I call them ghosties because they don't leave a footprint."

"They don't leave a footprint *in* an electronic system or don't leave a footprint *on* an electronic system?" Trevor asked, looking for clarification.

She smiled. "Most people wouldn't even think to ask that," she said, "but in this case I would go with *in* the system."

"So, you're saying that somebody, something, has accessed or has come here and attached itself to this energy."

"It's already gotten in," she declared. "I don't know how or why. I don't know if they downloaded something that would have set this off, but what I can say with certainty is that this feels … as if it was planned. It feels like deliberate sabotage, and it feels very much like a ghost."

"Okay, so that ghost term," Damon noted, looking over at her puzzled, "I gather that's a phrase you're accustomed to using."

"Yes, I guess so. It's when you have something that you can't find any tracks for," she explained. "I don't know if you guys understand what I mean."

"We would use the term *ghost* for somebody who causes chaos, then disappears without leaving a trace. Something you can't see."

"Exactly," she agreed. "So what you have here is an electronic ghost, but I don't mean electronic as in hardware. I mean electronic as in software—kind of."

Bullard's breath went out in a solid *whoosh* as he raised one brow and stared at her, then over at Damon. "But that's our specialty," he grumbled.

"Inside job," Reeni muttered, getting another glare from Bullard.

Damon studied her intently. "That's a fascinating concept, but I'm wondering … if you can see that energy, can you track it too?"

She pondered that and shrugged. "I can see that it's leaving this building." She looked around, as if literally seeing something. "I can see that it's attached to this server base and to that actual disk." Then she shook her head and took a cleansing breath. "Now, to see it past that point, I'm not so sure," she muttered, "because there's …" She hesitated, then winced and looked over at Trevor nervously. "You won't like this."

"We may not," he agreed, with a smile, "but we will deal with it, and we promise we won't shoot the messenger. Right, guys? Just say it, Reeni. What are you seeing?"

"It's characteristically male energy, and there's an awful

lot of … I want to say, *violence*, but it's more like *anger* attached to it. I don't always get emotions, but, in this case, I feel a cold and clinical perception, and then, every once in a while, rage spills into it."

Everybody stopped and stared at her. Meanwhile Trevor ejected that disk, holding it carefully.

She shrugged. "Yeah, I get it. You don't like anything I have to say, and it's hard to believe anything I have to offer." She nodded glumly at the others. "Why is it that I have such a hard time getting anybody to listen to me about what I see and what I don't see?"

"It's a fairly untested field, for one thing," Damon shared, continuing to study her.

"You're checking out my energy right now," she noted, watching him. "Do you see anything that says deception?"

"No, I don't. Not at all."

She nodded. "But what you're also not seeing is anything you really recognize. That's because I'm an anomaly in your world."

"I would have said that not too many more anomalies were possible, yet you're proving me wrong there," Damon noted honestly. "I don't have anything against new, different, or unique." He turned to the others. "I definitely have seen an awful lot more at Terk's place over these last few months than we ever expected to see. So I'm certainly not discounting anything Reeni has to say, but, because her line of expertise is so nebulous, it's much harder to prove." She nodded, and Damon circled back to where they started. "The question now though is this. … Reeni, can you track where this angry energy is coming from?"

She stared at him for a moment. "Do you have a map?"

His eyebrows shot up, and he turned to Bullard. "Do

you have any big maps here?'

"Come on." Bullard walked out of the room, headed off to a different corner of this building, and into a very large office area, with massive electronic screens up on the walls.

She looked at it all and smiled, as a world map appeared. "I do love this," she muttered warmly. She walked over to the map, closed her eyes, and seconds later stuck a finger almost blindly on the map. "Here," she declared. As soon as she pinpointed an area, everybody crowded around her.

Bullard stated, "But that's where we are now."

She double-checked. "Oh."

"What do you mean, *oh?*" Bullard asked, glaring at her.

"How was I supposed to know?" she replied, "I had my eyes closed."

"So, how is it that you chose that spot?" Trevor jumped in, seeing the frustration on the other faces.

"Because … I can feel it."

"So, the energy that you see coming out of the computer server on that one disk, you're telling us that you can feel the source of it."

"I can tell you where it's coming from, and it's coming from here, this area."

"Okay, so …" Trevor looked over at Bullard. "Zoom in on this map."

Bullard walked over to a wall unit, made several clicks, and up came a large map of the building where they stood and the surrounding area.

She walked over and put her finger on a specific point within this map. "Here. I can see it arcing from this point to where we are."

"Well hell," Bullard muttered. "I know that apartment building. My brother used to live there."

Immediately silence came from all around them, as Damon asked Bullard cautiously, "This apartment building can't be connected to you or your team, can it?"

"I trust my team," Bullard stated. "So I would never in a million years have thought so. Yet I wouldn't have expected someone to walk into my house and tell me that I had an electronic ghost either."

She shrugged. "I just haven't come up with a better name. Bottom line, somebody is trying to access your system, but he doesn't need a computer to do it."

"That's the part I don't get," one of the men piped up. "What do you mean, he doesn't need the computer to hack the system? How is that even possible?"

Damon and Trevor glanced at each other and then over at Bullard, who still frowned at them.

"God, this will be one of those woo-woo things you can't explain, isn't it?" Bullard asked.

"Yeah, it sure is," Trevor declared, with a smile. "It's one of those things that none of us can explain in a way that anyone can understand, even among some of us energy workers."

At that, Bullard glared. "That's even worse because, are you guys saying we have an energy worker gone bad, one of Terk's guys gone bad?"

Trevor shook his head. "No way. Not anybody on Terk's team or even associated with him. Yet you may have someone with some limited energy skills, or with some smoke-and-mirrors deceptions to give that illusion."

Bullard shook his head. "If it were just you two guys, I would sit here and argue until I was blue in the face, and you would do something stupid and prove to me that I'm wrong." He was oozing frustration now, and all three of them could see it. "Then I would give in and acknowledge that there's a lot of shit in this world I don't want to deal with and that you guys can handle any cases that have that crap. Then *she* comes along," he added, turning to glare at Reeni, "and there's no proof, there's nothing. What do you expect me to do now?"

She looked at him and asked, "You want proof?" She reached out a hand, snatched the disk from Trevor's hand, and popped it into Bullard's hand. "Tell me what's on it."

Everybody looked at each other for a moment, then one of the men grabbed the disk and walked over to another computer, and brought it up. "It's blank," he said in shock, turning to Bullard.

"What do you mean it's blank? That's the server for our satellite."

Just then all the phone lines rang, and even Damon's cell phone went off.

"What the hell?" Bullard roared. "What's going on?" He brought up his phone, and it was Levi.

Levi yelled, "What the hell is going on?"

"What do you mean?" Bullard asked in confusion.

"Your satellite's going nuts up there," he bellowed. "It's about to crash."

"No, no, no, no," Bullard cried out. He asked Levi, "Do you have any way to control it from your end?"

"No, I don't, but, if it's a computer systems problem, there should be a backup disk."

"Yes, where's that damn backup?" Bullard yelled, turning to his men, who were all scrambling.

As all that chaos was going on, Trevor watched Reeni. She stood in the midst of it all, as if a calm ocean. As soon as his gaze landed on her, he looked at her intently and asked,

"Can you fix it?"

She looked at him. "I think so. Do you want me to?"

"Yes, damn it. Why don't you step up and do that?" Bullard snapped, his gaze hard, fiery. "It would give a whole lot more validity to what you say you can do, but do it now."

"I don't know what I can do," she replied, almost irritated by his comment. "As you well know there are no clear-cut answers." Still, she returned to the server room and pointed. "Put the disk back in the server."

Without question, one of the men replaced the disk into the server and stepped back.

She closed her eyes, placed her hand over the top, and frowned.

Almost immediately Trevor felt an inner nudge. He walked over and placed his hand on her shoulder, feeling her energy surge into his, with a sense of power he didn't remember her having control of before. He called Damon over.

Damon stepped up and placed a hand on Trevor's shoulder, and with the three sets of energy plowing forward, Reeni did something Trevor couldn't explain, making all their hair stand up as the air filled with electrical crackles. Then their energy surged and stilled, and the weird crackling in the air stilled as well.

Finally silence once again fell over the room.

CHAPTER 4

"**D**ON'T LET GO," Reeni told Damon and Trevor, her hand still atop the server. "I really need to learn more about electronics, don't I?" she asked Trevor, with an agonized groan.

"Yep, you sure do," he agreed, with a smile, "if only to help explain what you're hearing, seeing, and feeling."

Bullard walked closer, his hand on his hips, looking as if he wouldn't take no for an answer and snapped, "What just happened?"

Levi came back online, appearing on the big screen in this room. "Looks as if you fixed it somehow, so I gather you found the backup?"

Everybody turned and looked at Reeni.

She sighed. "No, it wasn't the backup. At the moment I'm holding it steady, with the help of Damon's and Trevor's energy. So you other guys need to find that backup." She turned and glared at the other men. "Soon, people, so don't quit looking."

Realizing that something else had to be done here, the men were galvanized into action and scrambled very quickly. Half a minute later, someone shouted, "Okay, we've got the program back up and running again."

Trevor called back, "We'll let you know in a second if it'll hold or not."

She frowned at him.

Trevor nodded. "The three of us should reverse our link, as we withdraw our energy. Damon, you first. Now me. And, Reeni, disconnect from it," he said. "I'll hold you steady, if need be."

She smiled, and he watched as all their energy was uncoupled from the server disk.

When all the cell phones remained quiet this time, Bullard's men in the room gave a collective sigh. One guy shared, "Okay, we're still functioning. Levi, are you seeing it? Is everything okay?"

"Yeah, we have a visual. Everything looks okay now." Levi went silent for a moment, and then he exploded. "What the hell was that all about?"

Bullard groaned. "If I had answers for you, I would be a whole lot happier, but Terk's people tell me that what I apparently have is a ghost," he added, with a tone of disgust in his voice.

Levi repeated, "A ghost?"

"Yeah. You'll have to talk to Terk about that," Bullard grumbled. "I've got somebody here who says I've got an electronic ghost in my system, and now that we've seen our satellite nearly crash, I don't have a clue what to think." With that said, he stormed out of the room, looking more than pissed.

Damon walked over to the big-screen TV, so Levi could see him. "Hi, Levi. It's Damon. I'm over here with Trevor and Reeni," he explained. "She sounded the alarm, and she just stabilized the system, until they could regain control by rebooting it with the backup disk. But, yeah, we've got a problem here, and it's a problem that'll require our particular set of talents."

Levi shook his head. "Whatever that ghost is about, you keep him over there. We sure as hell don't need that problem here."

"None of us do, no matter where we are," Damon noted. "So, yeah, we'll get to the bottom of it."

At that, Reeni stepped in front of the screen and smiled. "Hey, Levi."

He stared at her. "Reeni, as in Tangerine? I haven't seen you in …"

She smiled. "You haven't seen me since I was little. It's been ages, I know."

"Yeah, but it's not as if I could ever mistake you, not even more than a decade later."

She burst out laughing. "Very true. … Unfortunately I don't think Bullard likes me much." She had such a sad tone to her voice.

Levi shook his head. "I don't believe that for a moment. You've probably completely confounded him, confused him, and destroyed his sense of calm, that's all. Give him a chance to adjust, and he'll be back in fighting form soon."

"Maybe so. I guess I should be used to it by now."

At that, Levi's face twisted in understanding. "No better at home, *huh?*"

"No, no better at home. It'll never be any better. You and I both know that."

"Sadly, if it's still not improved at this point, it's quite possible that things won't ever improve. In that case, you're far better off with a group like Terk's, who understand who you are and what you're up to," he suggested. "Keep that in mind."

"Yeah, though Terk didn't send me over here," she clarified. "I just showed up on Bullard's doorstep, without any warning."

He stared at her in surprise, then he started to laugh. "Honey, you are so lucky they even let you in. Those guys aren't known for letting strangers in to tell them about threats to their system."

"They didn't accept me until Trevor and Damon showed up, but I was right. Their electricity had been going crazy. I didn't help things though, as I have this tendency to just blurt out information. I don't couch the news very well, apparently."

He chuckled. "No, you don't have filters, or at least you never used to. I always really loved that about you because you are exactly who and what you appear to be. I would much rather deal with someone like that, than a lot of others in our society who aren't straightforward at all." They talked for a few more minutes, and then he ended the transmission.

She stepped away from the screen, feeling so much better. She turned around to see a half-dozen faces frowning at her, and, sure enough, Bullard was right in the middle of it.

"You know Levi?" he asked.

She nodded. "I do, but it's been a long time." She didn't elaborate. "I have friends all over the world, but I seem to be pretty good at making enemies too."

Bullard sighed. "I'm definitely not your enemy," he stated, "but you are challenging to anybody's belief system."

She nodded. "Yep, I sure am," she replied, without a second thought. She'd never been one to sugarcoat anything. "Apparently my parents think so too." Then she shrugged and smiled. "Sorry, I should be used to it by now, but that disgust or dismay, whatever you want to call it, it still takes a bit of getting used to."

Several women walked into the room just then, who had

clearly heard the whole conversation. One of them she recognized from earlier, Bullard's wife.

"Nobody has the right to make you feel less than who you are," Leia declared. "I'm not exactly sure what's going on, but, if you can help us in any way, we would all appreciate it very much."

Reeni smiled. "Thank you for that. … I don't suppose there's any more of that coffee, is there?"

From the far corner of the room, Dave laughed out loud. "Absolutely. The coffee's always on around here. Come on with me. Let's go get you a cup. Have you eaten?"

"No, I haven't had anything in a while," she admitted.

"It's been pretty intense, and I bet your blood sugar could use a boost. Let's see if we can find something for you."

"Thank you. If it weren't for these two helping, I might be in a very different state right now," she admitted, turning to Damon and Trevor. "Thank you for stepping up, both of you."

"You know, anybody in our business does that without question," Trevor shared. "You could have asked for it earlier."

She shrugged. "I'm not used to working with anybody. I don't do this work intentionally. It's just when that feeling becomes something that I can't ignore, I end up in these situations that are more foolish than sane, and people don't really understand or appreciate it," she explained, with a sideways glance at Bullard.

He stared at her as she walked past, heading toward the coffeepot. When Trevor came up behind her, he looped an arm over her shoulders, turned her slightly and gave her a kiss on her forehead. "Good job."

"Yet, all we did was postpone the inevitable," she muttered.

At that, Bullard must have heard her because he suddenly roared, "What?"

Her shoulders slumped, and she stared up at Trevor. "See? I have no filters. How do I ever get people to like me if all I do is say things that upset them?"

Trevor grinned. "In fairness, it is his security system. You put a stop to the oncoming disaster so, of course, he's a little upset to find that it's not over. It's hard to defend yourself against things you can't even begin to understand. He just wants his system to be working so his people are safe and to know this won't be repeated."

"Sure." She turned to Damon. "When you were attached to me, did you feel it?"

Damon nodded slowly. "I'm not sure what I felt, but yes." Then he shook, as if he wanted to ward off something. "I've never had that before."

"Never had what?" she asked curiously.

"That weird … electrical energy coursing through me, and the loud crackling, followed by that sense of openness, emptiness."

"Oh, so you got that much," she crowed in delight. "That's excellent, so you can tell Bullard that I'm not crazy."

Trevor grinned over at Bullard, who stared at Reeni as if she were something completely alien, which she was. "Just remember that she comes from the heart." Trevor smiled.

Now detached from his side, she found her way to the kitchen, where Dave made her a big salad and dished up some hot soup. As she sat there at the cozy informal kitchen table, inhaling the food, she still felt her energy draining quickly. Frowning at that, she ate a little faster but realized she was still losing the battle. She tried eating still faster yet again. When Trevor appeared, she groaned. "Can you give me some energy?" She moaned. "I feel as if I'm fading." He smiled, placed his hand on her shoulder, and she felt his energy surging through her. She straightened happily, then flared at him. "Don't give me so much that you're in trouble though."

"Doesn't happen that way, remember?"

"You say that, but it seems to work that way for me," she muttered.

Dave looked over at them inquiringly.

Trevor explained, "She lost a lot of energy taking on that energy jolt from the computer, so she's trying to eat faster to regain what she needs. So far, it's not working."

Dave stepped up and asked, "What kind of food does she need?"

Trevor turned to her.

She shrugged. "Oh, I would say protein would be normal, but starchy carbs would help too."

He turned and sliced thick slabs of ham on a cutting board and added bread. "I have potato salad here somewhere." Soon he brought that out of the massive fridge.

In a matter of minutes, she was completely surrounded by food, and, sighing happily, she went to town, eating some of all of it.

As the others came in, they stopped and took one look, amazed. Bullard shook his head at the amount of the food in front of her, plus the way she was digging into it all. "Good God," he muttered.

Trevor smiled and explained, "She burned through a lot of energy deflecting that intrusion, so, before she collapses, she needs some sustenance."

Bullard nodded. "Get her whatever she needs," he declared. "I certainly didn't mean to be less than friendly at her arrival," he conceded, with a headshake, "but some of this is pretty far out there."

"It absolutely is unusual," Trevor agreed. "That doesn't mean it's not valid."

"No, obviously it is. I'm just not sure how much of our world is ready for these things."

"Oh, I don't think it is," she mumbled around the food. "Most people don't see it coming and don't even want to think about it. I get it, but I'm not sure what I'm supposed to do with the information—other than tell you about it—not when I have it burning a hole in my brain."

"Why your brain though?" Damon asked, looking at her. "Do you have any connection to this person?"

She stared at him and then shrugged. "I don't think so, but I'm not sure. I don't know anybody who does electricity like this."

"Do you know other people with rare abilities?" Leia asked, her tone curious and yet not in any way judgmental.

Reeni considered that question for a moment and then shrugged. "I know people who can hijack cars, can get them started without keys, don't even need to hotwire them. A couple of them I've had to put in jail, which has been a little stressful for them, I'm sure. ... One guy could open safes without even touching the locks," she noted, with a shrug. "Of course, not everybody appreciates the fact that I can see what they're doing or can anticipate what their next move will be, so it pisses them off when they find out."

Trevor studied her. "Somebody opening a safe without touching it is an interesting possibility. That's just fascinating, when you think about it."

"Psychokinesis. Yet it's all just energy, right?" she stated, looking at him. "So, as long as they get the right vibration, the safe will open."

Trevor stared at her. "Yet you're telling me that you can't see a lot of this other stuff that's just energy."

She smiled. "Seeing it is one thing, but acting on it? … That's very different," she stated. "If I'm in the zone, then I can see a lot of stuff that I don't really understand and that I don't really work with. I saw a lot more when you touched me, and that really surprised me."

"That's what happens when you get around other energy workers," Damon noted. "The minute you work with somebody else, you can get a lot more energy, a lot more strength, a lot more awareness from it too, picking up more gifts." He looked down at the food in front of her and asked mildly, "Are you into sharing that?"

She looked up and smiled at Damon. "Absolutely." Then she frowned at Dave. "Did I take too much? I don't want to eat you all out of house and home."

"No, you're fine," Dave said, from the kitchen sink, washing up some pots and pans. "We keep things pretty well stocked around here."

With that, Damon sat down and started to fill a plate for himself.

When Trevor joined them, and everybody else just stood around and watched them eat, Bullard said, "This *energy work* really does affect you guys, doesn't it?"

Damon nodded. "It does. Sometimes more than others. I was surprised at this level today," he admitted, looking over at her. "That was a huge drain of energy."

She shrugged. "We stabilized the system." Then she stopped and chuckled. "It was more than just stabilizing. I booted him out, which might piss him right off." She frowned. "I'm not sure what else I was supposed to do, but sometimes I have a tendency to upset people when I do these things. I don't want to make you angry, Bullard, but he might come back more pissed off than ever."

As the room stared in shock, Bullard asked cautiously, not sure whether he would like the answer to his own question, "What does that mean exactly?"

She saw the look on his face and groaned. "If he's intent on doing damage here, he'll likely try another attack. I can't be sure though." She wondered if she should say anything more and then decided there wasn't a good reason to *not* share it. "If he does, it's likely to be much worse next time."

TREVOR WANTED TO laugh. It was so completely and utterly like Reeni to totally ignore them, while plowing through massive amounts of food. He nudged her. "You can't drop a bombshell like that and not explain yourself."

She blinked at him several times, then looked at the rest of them, staring at her. "Oh."

"Yeah, *oh*," Bullard repeated in exasperation. "A little more information, please."

"That would be nice," she noted, "but having already booted him out to save your satellite, I couldn't really get much more information, now could I?"

"And if you hadn't booted him out?"

"Your satellite would have fallen, for one," she stated simply. "So I guess I wouldn't have gotten any information anyway."

At that, Trevor burst out laughing. Bullard glared at

him, but Trevor could only smile. "Give her a chance to sort it out," he suggested.

Bullard groaned, then grabbed a slab of bread off the platter. "I don't know why I'm eating, except that my stress level is off the charts. So don't mind me while I munch." And he sat down beside her and tucked into the food too.

Trevor was a little surprised, but then remembered how it took people a while to warm up to Reeni. Yet, once they got there, they tended to collect around her. Trevor wasn't sure that Bullard was aware of it or that he even understood it was a possibility. However, as everybody else slowly took up seats in the kitchen, Trevor realized just how much power she wielded. And, all the while, she had no idea.

He looked over at Damon, who was even now processing the information in his head, an intent expression on his face. "Any ideas?" Trevor asked Damon.

"No, all I can say is that I think she is right. Somebody was utilizing energy to mess up Bullard's satellite, which is very important to all of you here, and to Terk and Levi too, since neither has their own satellite." Trevor turned to Bullard. "Did anybody *not* get a satellite because of you? Did somebody want to service the satellite, and you wouldn't let him? Did somebody want to go *halfsies* with you on your satellite or something like that? I'm just trying to understand why someone would target the satellite."

"Because it's the mainstay of our business," Bullard stated. "If they wanted to knock me off the business map—or off the physical map too, I guess—that would be one hell of a way to do it." He looked back at the map, up on the big screen in this room as well. "I'll head over to that apartment today."

"No, you will not," Damon declared in a tone that

brooked no argument.

Trevor hid his smile, as he watched the consternation flood Bullard's expression.

Bullard, not accustomed to being argued with, glared at Damon.

Damon explained, "Trevor and I will go. Maybe we'll even take Reeni with us, but we need to go in covertly and see what energy is floating around that place. We don't need you to go in there with a sledgehammer," he added, with a smirk.

Bullard continued to glare at him, but Damon smiled. "Yeah, I do remember what you're like, and this case requires a bit of finesse. In the meantime, you make a list of people with a grudge against you, as many as you can possibly come up with. Then your guys can run them down and see where they're at, what they're doing, and just what the mood is with them," Damon suggested. "We'll need those names, so we can take a look at them too."

"Do you care about the names?" Reeni asked him. "Or are you more concerned about the energy around the names?"

Damon smiled at her. "Very good. You got there quickly. So, yeah, that's exactly what we need, the names on paper so we can get a feel for their energy, an idea of their state of mind."

At that, Bullard snorted. "What the hell happened to our world if this is how you guys investigate?"

"It's not how we investigate," Damon clarified. "Still, we might knock off a few names from the list, without having to lift a finger, so we can move forward more efficiently," he explained. "We don't have time to waste before there's another attack." He looked over at Reeni. "Are you okay to come to the apartment?"

She nodded. "Yeah, I can do that. I don't think anybody will be there though." She stared off in the distance.

Damon nodded. "I don't think so either. Regardless we need to see the energy remnants."

At that, Bullard spoke up. "I'll go with you." His voice was determined, and there was no give in it.

Damon and Trevor shared a glance and nodded in understanding. Damon shook his head at Bullard. "One of your men can go—but not you."

Bullard glared at him.

"No, this is targeted at you," Damon snapped, "so you have to watch your home base. Send one of your men with us, and we'll stay in touch."

Bullard had to be happy with that. When his wife, Leia, wrapped an arm around his shoulders and smiled at him, he sighed. "Fine," he muttered, "but I would much rather be out there in the field."

"We all understand that because we all feel the same way," Reeni shared, a hard glint in her gaze. "This isn't the time."

"If this isn't the time, what time is it?" Bullard muttered.

"It's time for whoever this is to know that we won't just do what they want us to do," she shared.

"Will you stop them?" he asked, but no mockery was in his tone this time. There was almost a curiosity, as if to see what she would say.

"I will if I can," she said. "It also depends on how willing you are to let me into your system. I'll need complete access." The look of horror on his face had her laughing. "See? An awful lot is out there that you don't really know is happening." She pointed her fork at him. "Even the thought of letting me loose in your system is enough to give you the heebie-jeebies."

"*Heebie-jeebies*," he repeated, with an ironic tone, "is hardly a scientific term. Knowing you have no background or experience in electronics is enough to give anybody the *heebie-jeebies*," he declared, with an eyeroll.

"Yeah, but I'm not there to touch your electronics, not physically," she pointed out, with a sigh. "That's the part you must remember. I'm *in* your electronics energetically. I'm *one with* your electronics energetically," she said, "but I'm not physically touching your electronics."

And, with that brain twister, she went back to eating.

CHAPTER 5

TREVOR AND REENI were in the back seat of one of Bullard's vehicles, driving through town. Damon was at the wheel, with one of Bullard's men in the passenger seat. Trevor smiled at Reeni and asked, "Are you okay? Have you recovered from expending all that energy?"

"Sure, just trying to figure out what I'm supposed to do with my life. I can't go around knocking on people's doors, telling them they've got a problem, then spending days trying to explain it to them," she shared, with a groan. "It's a complete waste of my time and energy."

"It absolutely is," he agreed. "So, the trick at this point is to figure out what you need to do in order to get the validity that you need."

"And this is where you steer this conversation back to Terk, right?"

"Maybe. I can't speak for what Terk would necessarily want."

"Because he wouldn't know what to do with me, right?" she asked, with a sigh.

In the front seat, Damon just laughed. "Don't be so quick to judge him. Terk knows what to do with an awful lot of things that some of us have never even thought of. *Unthinkable* definitely describes this case and Reeni's gifts. So, just because Terk's never seen your talents before in anyone else, that doesn't mean he can't acknowledge that they exist or that they have value."

"Do you think he would take anything at face value though?" she asked. "Just think about the things that I'm asking people to accept."

"Terk has seen a lot in this world," Damon stated. "We all have, and those who have seen less are the ones we left behind."

"Except *this one* we brought along," she snorted, with a side look at Ryland, one of the men nominated by Bullard to accompany them.

"I can't say I've seen anything like what you guys are talking about," Ryland admitted. "It's pretty far out there, but I've always known something more was there. So I guess I'm a little more open to it than a lot of them."

At that, Damon looked at him. "Any personal experience?"

"Not so much personal experience, just a knowledge, a knowing that something more is going on around us. I've always had very strong instincts, and I think most of us who work in this field would say that as well. We have solid instincts just because you need to. Otherwise shit happens."

"Exactly," Damon agreed. "Shit does happen, and it happens a little too often in our world. So, anytime we can do something to give us a home-field advantage, it's definitely something we'll try for."

"Got it, and believe me that I am with you 100 percent. I'm just not sure what to do to make it workable though. Some of this stuff that you're talking about is pretty far out there."

She smiled and nodded. "It's out there, but, once you've been touched by it, there's really no going back."

Ryland nodded. "I can see that. I'm not sure it's as clear-cut as you might want to think it is, but I get it," he shared. "I definitely see, feel things at various times. Even back there, I could sense the energy in the room just jump."

"Okay, good." She smiled. "The more sensitive to energy that you are, the easier it is to get the people around you on board."

"And yet I'm not sure that I'm 100 percent on board myself."

"Nobody's 100 percent," she declared, "especially me. Every time I approach someone, I feel like a complete weirdo. Yet, if I don't tell people, then I'm in trouble because I haven't followed through." She shook her head, as if to ward off an unpleasant feeling. "I pay for it."

"In what way?" Damon asked her curiously.

"I can get quite sick to my stomach. I see visions I don't like and more. I feel this impending doom, and, if I don't try to help, something bad will happen. I could do without that in my life quite happily," she muttered. "No way can I deal with this on an ongoing basis. So, if I don't approach people, that impending doom takes over, and it sucks. ... It sucks big-time."

Not a whole lot the men could say to that.

When she suddenly felt a surge of energy around them, she called out, "Stop."

Damon pulled over and looked at her. "We're very close to the address but not quite close enough to walk yet."

"No, you're plenty close enough," she whispered, closing her eyes. "Can you feel it?"

"No, ... I can't. I'm not sure what I'm supposed to feel."

She frowned and shifted in her seat. "We're coming up against something very strong," she whispered. "As in *very*,

very strong, and I don't like it. It's wrong. It's … if you go in that building, there's a chance you won't come out."

All the men frowned at her.

She shrugged. "Wires and electrical energy is surging, looking for synapses to blow."

The men stiffened around her. "Jesus," Trevor muttered. "You know that's guaranteed to freak out everybody, right?"

She looked at him sadly. "I know. I know that, and I'm sorry. It's not what I would choose to tell people, but unfortunately something is definitely wrong out there." Her tone rose, almost in a panic. "It feels very much like the word I want is *blow*. I don't know if that means it's connected to a bomb or connected to something else, but something is very wrong with that building. No one should go in there, not at all. In fact, we should stay as far away as possible."

"But we can't tell anybody in that building to evacuate based on a *feeling*," Ryland blurted out.

She nodded at him. "I get that. I do, but that's what I'm getting. And that feeling is strong. … Something will blow."

"*Great*," Ryland muttered.

They sat in the vehicle for a long moment, until Trevor broke the silence. "Look, you guys. I have a pretty decent radar for something like that," he began, turning to her. "Let me go take a closer look."

She immediately shook her head. "No, you can't do that."

"We have to do something," he replied, staring at her. "You can't tell us exactly what we're looking at. We won't get any help from the authorities if we can't get at least something for them to go on. So I'll just go take a quick look."

She glared at him, and he smiled. "Remember that we all

have jobs to do. I can do this one."

"What if you're in there, and that whole thing goes up?"

"What if forty-five families are in that building, and it blows?"

She sucked in her breath. "Jesus." Pinching her eyes closed, she whispered, "Fine, but I may not be able to help you if you go in there."

"Do you think you can help if he doesn't?" Damon asked. "Because if you can do something from this distance, we need to know what that is."

She frowned. "I'm not sure I can do anything—except disrupt energy. That's what I do. I'm a disrupter. So, whatever is going on in there, maybe I can disengage it somehow or at least slow it down."

"Then do it," Damon ordered instantly. "Whatever it is, try your best to just disconnect it, and we'll deal with the fallout afterward."

"The fallout?" she repeated, with a harsh laugh. "It could be a permanent fallout."

"But, as Trevor already pointed out, it could be a permanent fallout for a bunch of innocent people who don't deserve any of this," Damon noted.

She sucked in her breath, then nodded. "Fine, but I'm just warning you that it might not turn out the way we want it to."

"What do you need?" Trevor asked.

She hesitated. "Some energy would be nice."

He held out his hand. She placed hers in it and asked, "Damon?"

"Go for it. Take what you need from me."

She looked at Ryland in the front seat. "So, if this gets a little weird …"

"Don't worry about me. I can do weird. I don't want to see anybody get hurt, and I really don't want to see a building blow up in front of us or go into one that's about to." He was clearly unnerved by it but holding his ground. "I'm not at all sure what you've got going on, but go for it." With that, he settled back.

"I might have to grab some of your energy too, Ryland," she added hesitantly.

"Don't know what that means either, but, hey, you do you."

She snorted at that and quickly shifted her focus, following the energy. She definitely felt it, could tell something was off about it, but it was here. She just didn't know how it was anchored here. As she closed her eyes, her energy raced up above their vehicle, higher and higher. She felt a stronger and stronger connection, until she came out at the other end and opened her eyes to see herself floating outside an apartment building. She frowned and muttered, "I'm outside the building. Trevor, can you see this?"

He just nodded.

"Can you see inside?" Damon asked her.

"Yes, all kinds of electrical wires are everywhere. I see the skeleton of the building, with all the electronics and wires. One area … is full of wires and canisters."

"Can you send a picture?" Trevor asked.

She snorted. "Do what?"

"Send a picture," he repeated. "Just send me a picture, an image of what you're looking at. See it and just snap it. We're one with the energy, so you can share that, and I should get it."

Not exactly sure what that meant or how she was supposed to handle it, she did as he asked and sent him a picture of what she saw. A sharp white blip filled the vehicle itself.

Ryland jumped a bit in the front passenger seat. "Okay, this is getting very weird."

"Yeah, you're not kidding," Damon noted, as he looked over at Trevor. "What's the deal with the picture? How can she do that?"

"That would be more about me. I have a photographic memory," he replied. "I'm hoping I can get an image off her energy as to what she's looking at. I would normally go look myself, but she's using my energy. With my energy mixed in with hers, and all of yours too, maybe we can get a sense of what is really there. I'm downloading the photo right now."

Damon stared at him in shock but had no time to process what he'd just heard by the time Trevor confirmed his receipt. "Got it."

She didn't dare ask him about what they'd just done or she would lose focus.

"Okay, Reeni, get back here," Trevor said. "Now we need to call the authorities and get that building evacuated. I'm not sure what kind of bomb it is, but definitely a bomb is in there."

"The problem is, if we evacuate the building, we'll risk triggering this guy," Damon shared, "and that's not cool either."

"It might not be cool, but at least that way people will survive," Trevor replied. "If we don't do anything, and that thing goes off, it'll be a one-way trip for everybody in there—and possibly for blocks all around. Now, I'm not sure it's prepped to blow. I'm not sure it's even a fully function-ing bomb, but I don't think we have a choice." He looked around at all of them and added, "We need the authorities out here now." He pulled out his phone and dialed the equivalent of the police in Africa.

BACK AT BULLARD'S compound, Reeni sat down with a hard *thump* at the long formal dining room table. A group of people waited, some looking at her curiously, as if wanting an explanation, but she was not prepared to give them anything. She looked over at Damon and shrugged. "This is your deal."

He snorted. "No, this is your deal."

"Not really," she argued. "I'm just the idiot who walked into this place with a warning." She shook her head. "I have to wonder where my brain was at."

"Clearly it was right on your shoulders and doing the correct thing," Leia stated, sitting down at her side. "And, no matter how they may feel, we all appreciate it."

Reeni looked over at her and nodded. "I don't think the city appreciates it right now."

"Did you really have to evacuate the entire apartment complex?" asked one of the women across the table.

"I didn't," Reeni clarified, "but the police did, and even they weren't very happy with the request."

"How do they feel now though?"

"Angry, upset, looking at me suspiciously. That's what happens when you're the bearer of bad news. Everybody looks at you to see if they can pin it all on you somehow," Reeni shared, trying hard to keep the bitterness out of her tone, but it wasn't easy. She did feel as if the cops were looking at her with suspicion, and it definitely felt as if they were trying to pin it all on her, even now.

"That's all right," Leia assured Reeni, with a determined

but soft tone, so as not to wake the sleeping child in her arms. "Bullard will handle it."

Reeni smiled at her. "It's nice to have such faith in your partner."

Leia nodded. "I do have faith in him, *absolute faith*," she declared. "If he can do anything to fix it, he will."

"There shouldn't be anything to fix," Eton stated, among all the other people at this dining room table, everyone studying Reeni's face. "You put out a bomb warning. Surely that's worth something."

"What it's worth," she clarified, facing him, "is a second look, at least according to the police."

"Right, but they won't find anything, so that is an is-sue," Trevor added. "The police need evidence to keep them off our backs, and we don't have anything physical to give them. It's the age-old problem that nobody wants to listen to psychics. Nobody wants to see or to deal with energy and things that they can't process with their five senses. Thus, that puts us energy workers in the position of not being able to explain what's going on because we're faced with that doubt all the time."

"That has to be hard," Leia muttered, with a nod. "It's one thing to be doubted some of the time but to know that, the minute you have to bring in the authorities, you'll always face that backlash? It makes you wonder about even going forward in the first place."

"Which is the problem," Reeni agreed. "I don't look like somebody who would have any credible information for people in charge," she noted, with a headshake, her huge halo of orange curls wafting around her head. "I really don't feel that I should have to cut my hair, or color it, or anything else to make me more acceptable to them," she shared, "any more than I feel I should change my sex just to satisfy the world's requirements either."

At that, some of the women laughed, and others nodded with a knowing look.

Leia agreed. "It's frustrating, isn't it? No matter how good you are at what you do, you're still judged because of the body that you're in. We understand that."

Reeni smiled. "The only reason you understand is because you have some experience with Terk and his team, and that experience is incredibly valuable."

"He helped us to find Bullard, after he went missing," said somebody off to Reeni's side.

So many people were at the table now that she'd lost track of them long ago. When Trevor walked over and sat down beside her, she felt an immediate sense of grounding, and it calmed her frazzled nerves. She sighed as she looked over at him. "You don't have to rescue me all the time, you know?"

He smiled, picked up her fingers, and laced them with his. "How about just some of the time?"

"Yeah, some of the time works," she muttered. She noted the looks everybody else gave them. Curiosity was bubbling from all corners. She shrugged. "No, we're not in a relationship. We did know each other beforehand though," she added, with a yawn. "There really isn't any explanation that I can give outside of the fact that we do the same work. He sees what it does to me sometimes. I should be happy he understands," she shared, with a smile at him. "God knows my family has no faith in me."

"Sometimes families are the worst," Leia said in understanding, "and can even be toxic. Sometimes they're the best thing ever. Sometimes it happens to be whatever you choose to make it." She held out the infant she carried to Reeni.

"Maybe," Reeni murmured, holding the baby gingerly, looking down at the little cherub, and whispered, "Now this baby is precious."

"Yes, indeed," Leia agreed. "Children help ground you. They help remind you of the reason why you're doing what you're doing. When they're not yours, it's harder to find a way to connect," she noted, "but, when they are, you'll do anything you can to keep them alive."

"Oh, it's not about *not* wanting to help out," Reeni clarified. "It's just so frustrating when the police are now investigating me." She turned and glared at Trevor. "Yet not him."

Trevor pointed out, "Terk has an awful lot more pull."

"So again, because you are part of Terk's team, you get a free pass?" she asked.

"Even if I'm *not* part of Terk's team," he stated. "In this case, I'm working with Terk, and that'll have the same desired result."

"Of course"—she sighed—"whereas I am a nobody."

He smiled. "Oh, you're definitely somebody, but you're an unknown. That's just how it is for now, but no need to stress about it."

She nodded glumly. "Fine, whatever. I haven't done anything in my sorry life. I'll just have a cup of coffee, and then I'll head out."

"Head out where?" Dave asked in concern.

She smiled at him. "I'm fine."

"Maybe you're fine," he conceded, "but you're doing all this to help us, and it's not as if you've been overwhelmed with hospitality."

She stared at him. "It's not as if I've been treated badly," she corrected. "I understand that I'm an outsider, and that's just the way it is." Looking around, she sighed. "After all, who wants a stranger like me, walking in your door, telling you all kinds of crazy people out there are after you? It's not as if you guys wanted to hear that today."

"If it's true, we absolutely do want to hear that." Dave's tone was clear, and the others chimed in their agreement.

"Sure, but when I told you—"

"But now we know that you're not a fraud. You're not here to blackmail anybody or for personal gain. We're still trying to figure out why you would even come here and put yourself through that in the first place."

She stared at him and sighed. "See? That's what I mean. People are always looking for that ulterior motive. *Why would you even help? What's in it for you?* Whereas there isn't anything in it for me."

"And that's why people struggle," Damon said, looking at her. "It's not about you. However, the world out there is so full of people focused on taking and stealing that nobody can understand someone who is focused on giving."

She didn't know what to say to that, but it did help to relieve some of her depression. As she looked down at her fingers linked with Trevor's, she realized that helped her depression too. She finished her coffee, while the conversation wrapped up around her, and then she took her hand back and stood up. "I'll head back to my hotel. I'll see you guys tomorrow, maybe."

Without giving anybody a chance to argue, she made her escape to the front door. When she got there, Bullard walked in. He glared at her, and she glared right back. "Where are you going?" he asked in that booming voice of his.

"I'm going back to my hotel to get some rest," she said.

"Damon and Trevor know how to contact me, if you need to." And, with that, she headed out to her car. She needed to escape, to destress alone. The day's events were catching up to her, and her gut instincts said, *Run!*

"Wait," Bullard called out.

She lifted a hand. "No thanks, not really into it. I need to take a load off, so I'll talk to you later, maybe." And she got into her vehicle and started to drive away. She only got as far as the gate, and it wouldn't open. She got out, looked at the gate, then back at the compound. Bullard walked toward her. Angry, tired, and frustrated, she bellowed, "Open the damn gate."

"And if I don't?" he asked.

"I'll open it myself," she snapped. "I won't be anybody's prisoner."

"What? Whoa, whoa, whoa," he called out. "You're not a prisoner."

"But, as I've gathered, I'm not that welcome either," she noted. "Believe me that I've gotten that message loud and clear, … a couple times already. I'm tired. I'm fed up. I want some peace and quiet, and I want to be alone."

"Peace and quiet, yes, alone, no," Bullard stated. "Not as long as this craziness is going on out there, you can't be alone. You can have some peace and quiet here tonight."

She looked at him in surprise. "Who was it who told you about the crazies?" she asked, her temper spiking. "Me. I told you. Yet it's not as if it mattered then."

"You're right, and I owe you an apology. I didn't take you seriously, and I should have, but again I didn't know if you had any valid information, not until I checked in with Terk would I know that. You can't get angry at people for taking time to confirm the information when you're completely unknown to me. We live in a world of betrayal, with murderers and terrorist groups," he explained. "So having you walk in wasn't something I was expecting or was prepared for."

"I understand that," she said, staring at him, "but I need to go get some rest."

His gaze narrowed, and he shook his head. "You're already exhausted and about to collapse."

"I would have gotten out of here just fine up until a few minutes ago," she pointed out, "but now you're trying to stop me, and that's starting to piss me right off."

"Just out of curiosity, what will you do if I don't open that gate?"

Maybe it was the snark in his tone, but more likely it was the challenge in his words that did it.

Furious, she turned and reached out a hand, aimed at the electronic gates. Immediately a series of snaps and crackles sounded, as if lightning had hit the gate, and it popped open. She glared at him and nodded. "That." She drove out, leaving him standing there, completely astonished.

TERK, FEELING THE *ping* of energy, picked up the phone and called Bullard. "Okay, what just happened?"

"You tell me," Bullard roared into the phone. "I can't believe she just did that."

Terk put it on Speakerphone, so the rest of the crew in residence could hear. People were always coming and going these days. "Calm down, and tell me what happened."

Bullard took a deep breath. "She just blew up my gate

and left."

His lips twitched. "She what?" he asked, trying to figure out just what that meant.

"You heard me," Bullard snapped.

"Why would she do that?"

Grudgingly Bullard admitted, "Because I asked her what would happen if I didn't let her out." There was little grace left in his tone.

"You mean, you threatened to not let her leave?" Terk asked in astonishment.

"I wouldn't do it against her will, but all kinds of shit has been happening, and she wanted to take off. However, I wasn't sure I was ready to let her go, not when she wasn't answering my questions," he explained. "I told her that she could stay here and rest instead, but she turned me down flat and demanded I open the gate. I guess I was being a little perverse and asked her what she would do if I didn't."

Terk pinched the bridge of his nose. "I presume she provided a visual response."

"Yeah, ya think?" he spat in disgust. "I'm not sure I can even fix the damn thing."

"No, you probably can't, at least not easily," Terk replied. "So, remember that saying about *don't play with fire?*"

Bullard muttered, "I had no idea she was dangerous."

"Really?" Terk snapped. "We all know that every person when cornered is dangerous, and, in her case, I would say a little more so, and that is unfortunate. You don't want her as an enemy, and definitely not when she came to help you."

Bullard quietened instantly. "What do you mean, in her case?"

"Her family tried to keep her imprisoned, had locked her up in a mental institution," he shared. "She swore she would never be locked up again."

"You could have told me that," Bullard snapped.

"Yeah, and when would I do that? When she came to your door, trying to tell you that you were in trouble, or when I sent over two men to help you out? Or maybe when you were off dealing with the apartment building where she found it completely wired for bombs?"

Terk had never lost his temper with Bullard before, yet he felt Terk's anger bubbling even this far away.

Terk continued. "She's tired. She's worn down. She's not sure of her welcome, and she's obviously going through a bit of a problem, and you pushed a button."

Silence came from the other end, until Bullard groaned. "And I suppose you'll say I deserved this."

"No, not necessarily," Terk conceded, with a chuckle, "but you should know yourself what it's like to come up against somebody who's decided to imprison you. That will never go over well. In her case, obviously she's more tired than we realized."

"Yeah, she's tired all right, and I think finding that bomb today really upset her."

"Why did finding it upset her?" he asked. "Seems that's a win, considering the alternative if she hadn't found it and if it had gone off."

"I think the police treated her more as a suspect than a hero, and she didn't take that well."

"Ah, well, that's an entirely different story," Terk muttered, "one that you should have been able to defuse easily and then placate her. She may have been tired, but she's not unreasonable."

"Yeah, I get that. I do," Bullard stated, "and I did talk to the police, but I wasn't thinking about defending her, more about why this would be happening to me."

"Now you have the men and the power there to fix the damn gate," Terk suggested, "and maybe next time you won't be quite so harsh, so she won't feel as if she has to explode your gate in order to get free. Honestly, at this point, I don't even know if she will return to your compound. I can't say I would really blame her."

"Shit," Bullard grumbled in disgust. "So, that's my fault too, isn't it?"

Terk wanted to laugh, but, aside from Bullard's obvious discomfort, it wasn't really a laughing matter at this point. "Listen. I know you're angry about things happening in your compound that you don't understand," Terk began, "and that is why you let people like my team in because it's our thing. Is she part of my team per se? No. Mostly because I've never really thought to bring her on. She's a bit of a wild card because of her past, though she doesn't know that I know about that, but I do. One of your best ways to deal with her and to keep her calm is by using Trevor."

"That's true enough. He does seem to have the magical answer to calm her."

"Has she been upset or irate or unable to stay calm?" Terk asked. "Or is it more about her feeling uncomfortable, trying to find her way in a situation that she really can't explain?"

"Yeah, the last one is probably more like it," Bullard noted in disgust. "Goddammit, Terk. Why is this shit never easy?"

"If it were easy, you wouldn't need people like me and my team," he replied in a gentle tone. "Look. I'll talk to her and see if I can settle her down."

"No, I need to do it. It's probably my fault to begin

with," Bullard grumped. "Will she even let me in, or will she send firebolts after me or some damn thing?"

"Let me know if she does because, in that case, I really need her on my team."

"*Right*," Bullard muttered in disgust. "Shit, if she can do that, *I* need her on *my* team."

"Oh no you don't," Terk argued. "You made your opinion about her abilities quite clear," he stated, still chuckling. "Let me talk to Trevor if he's right there. If not, tell him to call me."

"Will do." And, with that, Bullard ended the call.

TERK STARED DOWN at his phone and started to laugh. Celia looked over at him, as she walked in with a baby in each arm, handing off one to him. He smiled down at the cherubic face that reached up a hand and patted him on the cheek.

She asked, "What on earth was that all about?"

"You won't believe it," he stated, just as Sophia and Clary walked in, and he told them all what had happened. They stared at him in shock.

"She blew up his gate?" Sophia repeated in astonishment.

"The electronics apparently, and honestly, I don't blame her. Any one of us would have done the same. We don't imprison well," he declared, "and neither would Bullard."

"Even for him to joke about it, or to use it as a test to see what she would say or do, wasn't a good move. I don't know that I would have taken that myself," Clary shared, from the sidelines.

"So, Bullard just learned a very valuable lesson—hopefully."

Clary asked, "The question is, did he get it, though? We all love Bullard dearly, but we also know that some of this stuff flabbergasts him and what he tolerates from us, versus what he'll tolerate from somebody he doesn't know, is a very different story."

Terk sat back, enjoying the baby in his arms. "Look at it from his perspective, though. Bullard is trying to stave off what may well be an attack on his own home, not understanding who, where, why, or how, and he's fighting mad about it. Somebody he doesn't know showed up out of the blue, with all this crazy talk and a chip on her shoulder, and they end up averting a potential tragedy at that apartment complex, which had to leave Bullard rattled. Then she ends up blowing his gate to hell just because she can. And remember things are all different now that there are children at Bullard's compound. That changed everything and multiplied the responsibility he feels a thousand times over. He doesn't understand Reeni or what she can do. Plus, let's face it. She can be a bit of a loose cannon at times, which will definitely push his buttons."

"Maybe." Celia looked at him. "Do you think she's in trouble?"

"From Bullard? Never," he said. "In trouble from herself? Maybe. In trouble from her own impulsive nature and her own fears? Yes, but, to some degree, that's something we all deal with on a regular basis, isn't it?" He looked from each of his team to the other, and they all agreed.

Sophia nodded. "I don't think there's anything worse than knowing somebody has the power to take away your free will. And how come she's not on our team anyway?"

"Do you consider her stable enough to be part of our team?" Terk asked her.

She thought about it and then nodded. "I do. If she's got abilities, and new ones, we could really use her. Besides, we all have limits, and anyone can go haywire under pressure."

"Could we handle her?" Terk asked anyone in the room. "I can't really send her out on too many missions if she's erratic like that."

"I don't think that's erratic," Celia noted. "Emotional, yes, and maybe she was firing from the hip. However, she's clearly not used to having backup. She's not used to having support or somebody she can count on. That could really change her."

Cara walked into the room and added, "We also know that, when we're tired, when we're exhausted, we don't do a very good job of being the best humans we could be either."

Tasha was right behind her. "Yeah, we heard that on the Speaker call," she noted, rolling her eyes. "My sympathies are with her, and I get it. Bullard's probably very upset and doesn't understand what just happened, but, if he made even the slightest threat about not letting her leave, she was likely triggered and did what she needed to do. Maybe she could have done it differently. Maybe she didn't need to do it quite so quickly, with such a great show of power. Still, the reality is, Bullard will not underestimate her again. The fact that she found that apartment building with the bomb in it tells us a lot about what she can do. I get that everybody is probably worried about her stability because we certainly have seen people with our types of abilities simmering at the edge of sanity. Yet I think what she did, considering the fatigue, frustration, and hurt feelings from her lukewarm reception, was not completely out of line. Add in an interrogation by the cops, the fear of all that suspicion, and I'm on her side."

Terk agreed. He certainly wouldn't have tolerated any-thing like that either. He also knew that, despite his loud and blustery demeanor, Bullard would never have hurt her, but Reeni didn't know that, and that was the challenge.

"I know you believe he wouldn't have hurt her, and I don't disagree," Celia pointed out, looking at her husband, "but I'm on her side on this one. Just the thought of being imprisoned again is triggering for anyone who has been," she admitted, her tone dark. "I totally get where she is coming from."

Terk winced and reached out a hand. "That's not hap-pening. Never."

"You say that, … and I hear you," she noted, "yet that innate reaction happens before there's a chance to reason or to think logically. Bullard needs to know that he uninten-tionally laid wide open an old wound, and he'll have to work at it carefully to begin to build her trust. Whether he wants her help or not, she did go there to help him. She may have been unorthodox, showing up completely out of the blue, and she's definitely a bit dodgy, but her intention was to do the right thing."

"Whoever would have thought that Trevor would be involved?" Cara asked. The others looked at her, as Cara stared off in the distance and then nodded. "He really is, isn't he?"

Terk confirmed, "He is, and that is probably the biggest calming factor she has going for her. He appears to handle her brand of energy."

"Which I'm not sure that Reeni knows," Celia said, looking over at Cara. "Do you get that feeling?"

Cara shook her head. "No, I don't think she really does.

She acts as if she *feels* very much alone in this world. … I want to reach out and give her a hug."

"Yeah, me too," Clary agreed. "She's definitely been alone way too long." They both turned toward Terk.

He nodded. "That's her father's doing. When she started using her gifts, he couldn't handle it and had her institutionalized, … for many years," he noted. "Now, because of that, whenever people start doing any research into her background, that's what pops up, regardless of anything else she's accomplished in her life. That has stayed with her for way too long."

"And that's not fair," Celia said. "That's not her fault."

"No, it isn't," Terk replied, walking over and giving her an armload-of-baby hug, along with a gentle smile. "But we also know that nothing is fair in life and that this is just one of those burdens Reeni has had to bear. Should I have warned Bullard? Maybe so, but I honestly didn't think it was an issue."

"It wouldn't have happened if he hadn't threatened her," Celia said. "Shame on him."

"Yeah, well, he won't do it again," Terk noted, his lips twitching. "He'll be a while fixing that gate."

"But it's fixable?" she asked.

"It's fixable," he said, with a nod. "She could have made it much worse."

"So, this was her saying, *Back off. I'll do what I need to do, and you can't stop me.*"

"Something like that." Terk nodded in agreement. "Maybe not the subtlest methodology she could have used."

"I don't think *subtle* was part of her instinctive reaction," Clary stated. "I think it was all about being emotionally triggered, and that's the part that's dangerous."

"It is," Terk confirmed, "but I also think she's very trainable. However, if you guys don't agree or don't like what you're seeing, we'll have to reconsider. We can't collect injured and lone psychics who can't be redeemed," he noted, with a shrug, "no matter what they have for abilities. I get that's not a popular opinion, but, until somebody comes up with a solution, that's just where I'm at." And, with that, he gave Celia another gentle hug, while handing over the baby. "You may want to talk to Leia."

She chuckled. "I will. I'll see if she can get Bullard to calm down a bit."

"I think he's calming down, or at least he will once he gets his gate fixed," Terk replied, with a note of humor. "In the meantime, it might be best for him to just stay away from people."

And, with that, he headed to the office. He had a lot to fix himself.

TREVOR WALKED OUT to see if he could do anything to help. He never stopped Reeni when she was that determined and so in need of solitude. He had seen it before and knew better. So he wasn't responsible for whatever had just happened and had only felt some of it, but it had caused enough of a shock from the others that he'd gotten the picture pretty quickly. As he approached, Bullard glared at him. Trevor nodded. "Yeah. She's a bit of a wild card. Still, you might want to remember that she's a wild card who came to help you."

Bullard's shoulders slumped, then he nodded. "Terk just reminded me of that too," he muttered. "It's frustrating to see your family being attacked and to not know who, where, how, or why. Then to have somebody else turn up with abilities you don't understand was just too much. I was trying to get her to stay here, but she declined. Then I asked what she would do if I didn't let her out of the gate." Looking over at his wrecked gate, he stared at it and shook his head. "Anybody with that power—"

"Anybody with that kind of power, uncontrolled and crazy with anger at the world, is dangerous," Trevor stated. "But, for somebody like her, who came to help you in the first place, that was just a bit of a temper tantrum," he explained. "On the order of *Stop it, or I'll show you.* You'll notice that she didn't destroy the gate, and she had all the power in the world to do so. Believe me, because I felt it."

Bullard frowned at him and studied the gate. "Could she have?"

Damon joined them and laughed. "In a heartbeat. If she did this, then I'm sure she could have blown it sky-high. She also could have blown out all the electronics in your house," he added. "I don't think her gift is so much about energy as electricity, and she's very in tune with that field, as we've seen here," he pointed out, with a smile. "I've never seen anybody do that."

"Yeah, but is that because they can't, or because they don't?" Bullard asked.

"Most of the time it's because they don't," Damon replied, with a smile. "Most of the time they don't get so pissed off that this is the end result."

"*Great,*" Bullard muttered. "I'll be the butt of a joke for this now, won't I?"

"No, because I don't think anybody thought she could do this. Obviously it was a harsh reaction, but maybe that's a sign for you to be more respectful. She had a harsh child-hood."

Bullard nodded. "According to Terk she was institution-alized by her father, who wouldn't listen to anything she had to say. So, she reacts harshly to feeling imprisoned."

"Ya think?" Damon quipped, eyeing him. "I hadn't heard about that, although I've heard rumors of something ugly in her past. I can't say I'm surprised though. Her father's a jerk." Bullard just stared at him, and Damon went on. "He's a billionaire dude."

"Yeah, a billionaire dude who's a complete asshole," Trevor noted.

By the looks of it, he knew far more than they did.

Trevor continued. "He has absolutely zero love for his own daughter. Once it became apparent that something was different about Reeni—not even different in a bad way, just that she was different—was all it took. She wouldn't be the daughter who grew up to be the trophy wife, who her father planned on marrying off to some business associate to consolidate their commercial relationships," Trevor explained.

"I hadn't heard specifically about the institutionalized event," Damon noted, "although it makes perfect sense and aligns with everything that I do know. I should have already put that together. ... It still doesn't change the fact that she's very powerful and knows something's going on here. I just don't know if she'll be willing to work with Bullard anymore."

"No, probably not." Bullard ran a hand through his hair. "I need to go talk to her, don't I?"

Such a note of resignation filled his tone that even Damon had to smile. "If you want her to come back and help, yes. If not, then it doesn't matter," he replied. "Can we do it without her? Probably. It just depends on if this is how you want to leave things, and that's up to you." Damon shrugged. "I don't think anybody on your team will have a problem with it either way."

"Oh, they have a problem all right," Bullard said. "I can tell you that the women are definitely pissed at me."

At that comment, the men just nodded.

"Now *that* we can see," Trevor noted. "So, you decide what you want to do. In the meantime, I need to go after her and ensure she's okay." Trevor looked over at Damon, who nodded.

"You do that. We don't want her to be any more adversely affected by all this than she has to be. The fact is, the police did find a roomful of bomb-making equipment in preparation for a major attack of some kind, and we don't want to lose sight of that."

"Right." Trevor walked over to his rental, lifted a hand to Bullard, and added, "I'll talk to you in a bit." And, with that, he pulled out and went through the gate that nobody would control or close for quite a while. As he drove out, he called out to the ethers, *Reeni, I'm coming. Don't be upset. I'm just letting you know that I'm on the way.*

No answer came, of course, and he wasn't surprised. She was definitely on the stubborn side. As he considered what he knew about her father, it made sense. He'd only met the man once and had been deemed not good enough to warrant a greeting or any attempt at a conversation. Arrogant bastard.

He was clearly an asshole, and Trevor was totally okay to let him do that on his own. The world was full of them, and Trevor didn't need to deal with them himself. Yet now he felt a pull to step in, as Reeni needed to know that someone would support her on this. As he drove toward the city, he realized he had no idea where Reeni was staying.

He quickly phoned Terk, and, when he got Sophia instead, he asked, "Do you know where Reeni is staying? I'm heading to check in with her and to ensure she's okay."

"I have no idea. I assumed she would be staying with Bullard."

"She could have, I'm sure, but I don't think she was ever invited," he explained, "at least not until the conversation involved whether or not Bullard would open the gate. She left here pretty upset."

"I heard," Sophia stated, "and, just for the record, my sympathies are with her. I love Bullard too, but he blew that deal totally. What was he thinking?"

"Oh, don't worry. He's regretting his choice of words already. I just want to see that she's okay."

"I'll get back to you. Give me a few minutes." With that, she ended the call.

Trevor knew she could probably check credit cards for hotels close by within a few minutes, which would work, unless Reeni was staying under the radar and paid with cash. If she was trying to avoid her father, credit cards might be something she would avoid using. As he drove closer to town, he wondered if he could just follow the spray of erratic energy.

He definitely heard a distinct hum in the air, a weird buzz. He didn't know if it was her or if it was something else entirely. When Sophia phoned a few minutes later with the name of her hotel, Trevor realized he was nearby. He stared up at the building rising in front of him, as he pulled into the parking lot, wondering at his ability to home in on Reeni's energy.

"Are you there?" Sophia asked.

"Yeah, I am. I'm pulling into the hotel parking lot and was pretty well here already."

She laughed. "You didn't need me after all," she said in a teasing voice. "Sounds as if you're attuned to her all on your own."

"Maybe. That's certainly something to consider."

"Just don't overthink it," she said. "Right now, a definite sense of need is coming from her corner."

"I know. I feel it too."

"Good. Treat her nicely." With that, Sophia ended the call.

He found it odd that Reeni had picked up some very strong defenders so quickly. A few detractors too, but only in the sense that they didn't know quite what to do with her. Trevor understood that, but her latest move with the gate wouldn't endear her to some people. They'll just look at her with more fear than anything else at this point, worried that she might be out of control or might do something that would upset other people as well. It was one of the problems that arose when you did demonstrate that you could do something that defied scientific explanation. However, he also agreed that she didn't have to tolerate that behavior from Bullard or from anybody else. It would be interesting to see how this moved forward.

If the police wanted to talk to her, Trevor would have to coax her to go in and take care of that, before they told her that she could be hauled in for questioning if she didn't show up. That wouldn't sit well with her either, though it wasn't fair that they always went after the messenger. He parked, remembering the room number she had been assigned, thankful that Sophia had found that for him, and walked up at a steady pace.

When he got to the room, he sensed a strong *stay the hell away* energy emanating from inside. With a sigh, he knocked anyway and called out, "Let me in. It's just me, and I came alone."

Maybe it was the fact that he was alone or maybe that she was tired and worn out, but she opened the door and glared. He gave her a crooked grin. "May I come in?"

"What? You mean, you'll ask?" she snapped in a hard tone.

"Absolutely. Just like you, I don't want to be anywhere I'm not welcome."

She hesitated at that, then opened the door and stepped back.

He quickly walked in. As she closed the door and turned to face him, he didn't say anything and just opened his arms.

She shook her head and jutted out her chin. "No," she snapped. "I don't need a hug."

"We all need hugs," he replied, "especially me."

Her eyes widened at that, and, when he wiggled his fingers, she walked into his arms and gave him a hug. But even as he accepted the hug, he was generously pouring soothing energy into her soul. A good minute later, the dam finally broke, and she ended up bawling into his shoulder. He never understood why, but something to do with working with energy often made women cry to release the strain, the stress, or maybe just the electrical overload. He didn't know for sure, but he'd seen it happen time and time again.

When the tears finally stopped, she stepped back, looked up at him, and muttered, "I wasn't expecting that."

"I was," he said. "It's one sure way to release some of the anger, stress, and frustration."

"By crying?" she asked, with a mocking note. "Just makes me look even more helpless to the rest of the world."

"It doesn't matter how you look to the rest of the world," he stated. "Believe me that Bullard is feeling pretty badly for what he did."

She snorted. "I doubt it. He seems an awful lot like my father."

"That's not fair to Bullard. Your father is a complete bastard. Bullard is a lot of things but nothing at all like your father."

Startled, she looked over at him and then burst out laughing. "Sorry, I forgot that you'd met him."

"I have," he stated, with feeling. "Definitely not the warm and fuzzy father figure everybody should have."

"I don't know that anybody ever gets that," she noted. "It seems as if the men I see out on the streets just turn into these complete assholes once they're married and have kids. Or else I never have a chance to meet the ones who appear to be kind, caring, and intuitive," she added, with a shrug. "Maybe they don't even really exist."

"Maybe not," he said, with a shrug. "Yet Bullard is a good father, and he's a great team leader, and he cares very much about what happens at his compound. The fact that somebody was doing this to his place, without his even knowing about it, is why he's so very angry. He's very protective, and I think it rattled him that someone got that close, and he had no clue. They say he's always been that way, but even more so now that he's got a family."

"I can understand that," she replied, "but I sure didn't expect to have it blow up the way it did."

"No, and he didn't expect you to destroy his gate either."

Her lips twitched, and she nodded. "Of course not, but he shouldn't have made me feel as if I needed to prove that I could. I shouldn't have fallen for it either. That's the part I'm really pissed about. But, every once in a while, I just get fed up with people always judging, never understanding, and never accepting."

"Yet you also know that if you saw this for the first time …"

"I know, but that doesn't make it any easier." She was now glaring at him. "So, if you came here to preach, the door's behind you."

He chuckled. "I'm not the preaching type."

"No, you never used to be," she said, looking up at him curiously. "What are you doing here anyway?"

"I came to see if you were okay."

"I'm fine. Now you can leave."

He knew the prickly exterior and the fake frustration hid a very soft and wounded interior. So he just ignored her and sat down in the spare chair at the small desk. "Do you want some coffee?"

"Of course I want coffee," she muttered, "but nobody said I want coffee with you."

"No, but, … oh well." He reached across the desk, grabbed the hotel phone, and ordered coffee from room service.

"It's three times the price," she complained.

"Yes, but you're not prepared to go outside and to interact with the public, are you?" He watched the shudder ripple through her body, and he nodded. "That's what I mean. So coffee from room service is perfect right now, even at three times the price."

She slumped down on the bed and stared up at the ceiling. "I shouldn't have let him get to me."

"You shouldn't let anybody get to you," he clarified, "but since nobody is perfect … we're all on a journey. We're all working on figuring this out. You have abilities you don't really understand or have figured out how to make good use of yet. Thus, when people doubt or anger you, you have a tendency to react. This is a learning curve."

"*Great*, you make me sound like a pubescent teenager," she muttered.

"When it comes to energy, yeah. … We're all teenagers, so that's not even a bad analogy," he teased, with a cheeky grin.

She sighed. "I didn't hurt him, did I?"

"Just his pride, and he's got plenty of that, so I wouldn't worry about it."

At that, she laughed. "That he does. It's just the way he said it, as if he wouldn't let me out," she explained. "Just hearing that tone again makes me angry even now. He sounded like—"

"Your father, I get that. But maybe you should just try to understand where Bullard was coming from, why it happened, and it'll make it a little easier to walk past."

"I walked right past it when I smashed his gate. He'll have fun fixing that."

"It's what he does, and he's an electronics expert himself, so no worries there. He'll get over that."

At that, she stared at him. "Oh, so that'll just make him more pissed off about somebody getting in his system."

"Exactly," Trevor agreed, "but that's what I mean. Events are happening in his world that he didn't know about. He's trying to protect his team and now his young family as well. So, from his perspective, … he failed."

"How could he fail if he didn't even know about it?"

"Exactly, but, when you're somebody like Bullard, you expect to solve everything, and when you suddenly can't, and somebody can breach your home base, … it's terrifying, and he feels out of control."

"Particularly when this young carrot-topped Tangerine can do something about it," she added.

"Carrot-topped?" he replied, with emphasis. "A girl walks into his place, with this crazy tale, and then manages to prove that she knows something that he should have known—or at least he feels he should have known—just makes him very irritable."

"Yeah, well, I guess I have a temper myself." She stared up at the ceiling. "I didn't really expect to have it come out in this instance. I really was just trying to help," she said, looking over at him. "It seems as if that always goes wrong."

"It doesn't always go wrong," he corrected, "but a lot of the time? … Yeah, I can see how that happens."

"Back to that whole thing about not having Terk behind me, *huh*?"

"Having Terk behind you would definitely give you some validity, but you've never been someone to wait for somebody else to blow your own horn," he noted, "so validity isn't necessarily what you're after."

"Isn't it?" she asked. "Don't we all want validation? It solidifies that I can do this."

"You already know what you can do. It's validation that you have the same, if not more, abilities than other people and have a right to be you," he explained. "Yet the kind of validation that you are enough and that who you are is okay all has to come from inside you, and no team can provide that for you."

She stared at him for a long moment. "I wasn't expecting a self-help talk."

He smiled. "That's good. I wasn't expecting to give one either. It just seemed you needed to be reminded of that."

"What? That I'm okay, that I'm a whole person, not bits and pieces of my father?"

"That you are a whole person, that you're a valued person, that what you offer is also valuable," he reminded her. "No matter how much we don't want to acknowledge it, there will always be people we may not want in our life, yet are there for a reason," he shared, "and this may be one of those scenarios."

"My father used to laugh at me and would say almost the exact same thing, about not letting me out of the house. What could I do about it back then?" she asked. "So when Bullard said basically that ..." Her shoulders slumped. "It wasn't very nice of me, was it? Now I feel bad, and I really don't want to."

"Don't even worry about whether it was nice of you or not," he replied instantly. "You reacted, and, while we may wish it had been less volatile and damaging, it's over."

"Yet it's not over for anybody else," she argued. "Not for Bullard, not for me, not for the people who have to fix that gate, not for those people who will always look at me differently now. I try so hard to be normal, and then ... something like this happens, and I realize just how very abnormal I am."

"You're not abnormal," he declared. "You have an affinity for electricity, even though you don't really understand the workings of most electronics."

"Not quite true. I worked hard to learn," she stated. "I really did, but it seemed as if the more I learned, the more I lost in terms of learning. I know that sounds pretty stupid, but it just got so confusing because everything I was picking up was more energetic. As if my instincts were messing with the facts."

"Maybe focus on learning enough jargon so you can have a conversation with people in this field. Then maybe you'll realize you have no need to blow up gates to make a point."

"Which I thought I did," she declared, with a pointed look at him.

He nodded. After a moment he said, "Bullard probably needs a little bit of time to fix his gate and to calm down, and you need a little bit of time to calm down yourself. Other than that, I'm not sure there is any need for anybody to do anything."

"Do you think I should apologize to him?" she asked.

He looked at her steadily. "Do *you* feel as if you should?"

She shook her head. "No, I don't."

"Then don't," he said. "You need to understand what happened, why it happened, and go from there. You're not beholden to him. You went to him of your own free will, and, if you don't want to go back and talk to him, that's fine."

"No, that's running away," she murmured.

He gave her a ghost of a smile again. "In some ways, yes, but maybe that's what you need to do. You have to figure out what *you* need and go from there."

She fell back on the bed and muttered, "I need food."

"Now that I'm not surprised about." He chuckled. "Did you order anything?"

"No, of course not," she muttered, rolling her eyes. "My temper was keeping me full for quite a while, but now that's fired in the wrong direction," she noted. "I don't have anything here to eat."

"Okay, do you want to go out?"

"Not when we just ordered coffee." She looked at him sideways.

"But we could order room service."

She winced. "But it's so expensive."

"It is, but it's also convenient," he stated calmly. "And, right now, maybe convenience is more important."

She didn't appear to know what to say to that and just stayed quiet.

When a knock came on the door, he stood. "Let me get that. It'll be the coffee." He opened it up and brought the coffee inside, then asked the waiter how long it would take to get a room service meal.

"The kitchens aren't backed up right now," he replied, "so, depending on what you order, probably twenty or thirty minutes."

With that, Trevor smiled, and nodded. "Okay, we'll phone in an order here in the next few minutes." Armed with that information, he headed back into the room and served her a cup of coffee in bed. "Food can be here in half an hour, so let's find the menu and order something."

She reached over and grabbed the room service flyer. "You really think it's worthwhile?"

"It doesn't matter whether it's worthwhile or not," he said, eyeing her curiously. "You need food. You must have burned through a ton of energy blowing up that gate," he pointed out, with a note of laughter. "Even I know that you've got to be running on empty."

"It was stupid," she muttered. "I shouldn't have done it."

"Don't start crashing that wonderful sense of *hard-done-by-ness* that you have," he suggested, with a smile. "You did what you needed to do at the time. Now let it go."

She groaned. "Now I feel as if I should apologize."

He looked over at her and nodded. "If you still feel that need in a while, I am sure you'll get the opportunity, but you might want to give Bullard an opportunity to apologize too."

She stared at him and then laughed. "Somehow I don't see that happening."

"Bullard is not your father," he stated, his gaze watchful, looking for any nuances in her facial features that indicated she heard what he said. "Don't make the mistake of confusing the two."

She stiffened and glared at him, but he stayed firm. Finally she relented and admitted, "I guess I am confusing them, aren't I?"

"I think anybody you encounter with a forceful personality who questions you in some way or who otherwise tries to stop you from being you will always get that side look," he murmured, "and that's okay. You just have to decide which of them you'll let into that wonderful world inside your head," he stated. "And, if Bullard doesn't get a pass inside, then Bullard doesn't get a pass. Just don't knock him because you can't stand your father."

She glared at him and then shifted up against the headboard. "Are we not ordering food?" she asked pointedly.

"I am. I don't know about you," he quipped, with a smile. "You could have stayed at Bullard's and got food, and that would have been free too. Dave is a mean cook as well."

She sighed. "I was starting to get very drained there."

"A lot of people live and work there, and you're not used to being surrounded by all that many people."

"No, I'm not," she agreed. "Sometimes a lot of people is okay, but there was definitely that *off* sense."

"*Off* as in off with the people there, or *off* as in you were tired?"

She shrugged. "I don't know. I didn't really give myself a chance to sort it out."

"Because you realize that there's always a chance—though I'm not saying it's a big one—but, with something like this, we always have to consider the possibility that it's an inside job."

"Of course. That's what Bullard's thinking, isn't it?"

"I'm sure it's something he's afraid of, and he has to take a closer look at everybody he lives and works with, and nobody ever wants to do that," Trevor stated. "Same thing with Terk and his team, who are very close. And same thing with Bullard. He and his team are close as well."

"But haven't they had a bunch of new people join in?"

He frowned and stared at her, as he sipped his coffee and nodded. "Yes, he has. So did you get an odd feeling from one of them?"

She snorted. "I got an odd feeling off practically everybody there, but mostly because I felt as if I had to defend myself. … That whole *nobody knows me* element, *so they must be judging me* thing."

"Which is why it's interesting you went up there in the first place."

"Yes, it is." She nodded. "It was mostly because of the babies."

"Ah," he muttered. "Leia and the children got to you."

"Not just them, the others too. There are other pregnant women," she declared. "There seems to be an awful lot of pregnancies going on."

"Also an awful lot of that at Terk's place. I'm not so sure about Bullard's."

"It's there too," she declared, with a shrug. "Again, it's got to be electrical, doesn't it?"

"It's energy," Trevor corrected. "It doesn't have to be electrical. It's just energy."

"And yet, to me, it's electrical."

"I think we're just splitting hairs."

"Maybe I want to," she stated argumentatively, glaring at him.

He smiled. "Then you argue all you want. I'll just chill for a bit and relax." With that, he settled in his chair, a cup of coffee nearby, and sent Damon a text message.

"What are you telling them?" she asked.

"That I'm here with you and that you're fine. Believe it or not, everybody is quite worried about you."

Her eyebrows shot up at that. "Why?"

"Because not all people are assholes," he said. "And people care about you. They care about what happened, what is happening, so there'll be a lot more people than you're expecting in your face now." She winced at that, and he nodded. "That's what happens when you get into other people's lives. Then other people get into your life. You can slam the door, but you can't keep them all out."

"I could if I wanted to." He just looked at her, and she groaned. "Fine, that was a childish thing to say."

"It was an *I'm still angry at my father* thing to say," he pointed out. When she glared at him, he shrugged. "You know me. I'll call it as I see it, whether you like it or not."

"I don't know you all that well," she said, staring at him. "The person I do know was someone I didn't think was this developed."

"Of course not, any more than you were," he said, with a grin. "We're all coming into our own abilities, and that makes a hell of a difference."

"I'm not sure I like it," she muttered.

He grinned. "Maybe not, but it's right there in front of us, and that's what we have to work with."

"Sure," she muttered. "Easy for you to say."

"No, not so easy for me to say," he declared. "I don't have the same history, but we all have a certain amount of the past that we don't really want to discuss or to deal with. Everybody has something in their past. I don't know anybody who got through life unscathed."

"And yet it shouldn't be this marathon," she said, staring at him. "It shouldn't be a case of, *Wow, you survived.* It should be a whole lot easier, a whole lot nicer on us."

"Maybe if we weren't always alone, always bucking the system, always trying to do something that other people didn't particularly want us to do, maybe it would work out that way," he noted in exasperation. "Yet, so far, it appears that almost everything we do is exactly that, bucking the system, trying to stop people who are assholes, trying to do something to help others who don't believe in us and our gifts." He held up a hand as she started to contradict him. "And, yes, that's still what I'm doing. I don't even work for Terk, but he knows me, and he sent out a beacon, looking for workers."

"I felt that," she murmured. "However, I was pretty sure he wouldn't want anything to do with me."

He looked at her curiously. "Why? Are you really thinking Terk couldn't see past your father?"

"I'm thinking that he probably doesn't want a wild card," she noted.

"Will you always be a wild card?"

She stared at him and shrugged. "I have no idea what I am, really," she shared, her tone soft and contemplative. "Sometimes I think my father was right, and I should have just stayed locked up."

"Don't," Trevor snapped. "Don't ever think that, much less say that out loud. Whatever was going on in your father's mind was his problem, not yours. He made it your problem, and he was wrong. You're a good person, and you don't deserve what he did. The truth is, he didn't deserve to have you in his life," Trevor declared. "So just ditch all that."

She snorted. "You make it sound as if it's something I can just pull out of my brain and get rid of with a snap of my fingers," she said angrily.

"I know that Terk has energy healers he works with all the time. Plus, some of his people are married to some very incredible healers as well. Some of these people … could help you get rid of this baggage."

She blinked several times, processing that information. "What a thought, to think of a healer going into your brain and pulling out all those unwelcome memories." She shook her head. "That's a level of trust I don't think I have."

"It's a level of trust if you're expecting them to invade your mind to pull out those memories. However, if you will do the work yourself, there's much less trust required. Anyway, that's all a discussion for later. Right now, we need food, and we still haven't managed to order it."

"No, because you went and sat down in your chair," she said, tossing the menu at him.

He took a glance at it and announced, "I'll have burgers and fries."

She smiled. "That's almost cliché. You always order

that."

"I thought you didn't know me that well," he teased.

She rolled her eyes at him. "I do know you somewhat," she replied. "I could have picked out your menu choices from a mile away."

"So why didn't you?" he asked, with a yawn.

She frowned at him and yawned herself. "Will you fall asleep here?"

"Maybe," he said cheerfully. "You got a problem with that?"

"Maybe," she snapped, glaring at him. "It is my hotel room."

"Right. So you want me to get my own?" he asked. "Order lunch or dinner, whatever it is, will you? After that, I'll have a five-minute nap, so that I can get up and leave your fine establishment." He made a fake bow to show off, and she laughed, then quickly ordered the food.

He felt the burn starting to hit, and he needed just a little bit of time to recover. As he closed his eyes, he whispered, "Will you watch over me?"

"Of course," she murmured, her voice equally soft. "You watched over me, so I'll watch over you."

He gave her a quick thumbs-up, closed his eyes, and drifted off.

CHAPTER 6

REENI STARED AT this man who she knew somewhat, though not as well as she wanted to, as Trevor crashed on the chair across from her. Food would be coming soon, but he'd dropped his phone against his chest and had basically powered down. It was a fascinating process, and he'd done it so quickly and efficiently that she realized how adept he was at this. Maybe he had had years of practice.

She should cultivate that herself. She certainly needed to figure out how to stop the drain of energy, particularly when it decimated her so much, as it had today. She didn't know whether it was finding the bomb site, just that overload of information, or the final confrontation with Bullard, but something had hit her sideways. Finding out the cops were on her case, hearing the conversation and listening to them basically accuse her of having insider knowledge, had just finished her.

If she was trying to help people, why did the world continuously turn around and hit back at her with crap like this? She never understood that, unless it was because she was doing the wrong thing, and that was something she had wondered about time and time again. Yet, when that urgent feeling came across as being something she needed to do, it was impossible for her to do anything differently. What was she supposed to do when she knew an attack was happening?

The problem was, by the time she explained herself to people, either the attack was already happening, had happened, or they weren't even interested, maybe weren't even around after the fact, or argued that she should have done more. She always figured she needed to do more, and honestly, she hadn't had any other situations quite like this one. She hadn't realized who Bullard was, but she'd certainly recognized the amount of power at his compound.

Would it have changed anything? No. Even now she wondered at the temerity that allowed her to go up to a stranger's house and to tell him such a thing. The fact that they were in chaos and were trying to stop a complete outage hadn't helped because it was almost as if she had brought it with her. She pondered that, but surely that wasn't anything that she was doing. Similar things had happened around her before, but, as far as she was concerned, that was because of her energy. Seems it was pretty easy to mess up all kinds of things for other people with energy.

She wasn't very good at starting anything, but she certainly could stop things. And, in the case of the gate, could blow up electrical things. Not exactly tricks for parties—or at least not for the homeowner. Anybody attending would probably think it was the best, as party tricks go anyway.

She groaned as she got up and paced around the room. Whatever food was coming would be here relatively soon, but, in the meantime, Trevor needed the break. Whatever was coming would be big and ugly. She didn't want to be involved, but there was no way to get out of it now. She was involved whether she wanted to be or not. As she sat down again, she sent out a request for energy to see if anything reached back.

There was nothing. Absolutely nothing. Not for the first

time she wondered if she had imagined the original rush of energy coming to Bullard's place. But that was impossible, wasn't it? Surely she couldn't have made this up. One of her worst fears was that she was doing something to bring these things into existence. It shouldn't be possible, but that didn't mean that it wasn't possible. Because she was the only one who could really feel it, she always felt as if she was doing something to bring it all on. Not fair, not even realistic, but, if she was somehow triggering it, that would be bad news.

At the same time, how could she know who and what was going on in this craziness? If she was triggering it, was somebody else using her energy to launch these attacks, or was it something to do with her energy that made everything go on the fritz? No, she had sensed it coming toward them, to that address, in a big way. It hadn't been hard to follow the trail of energy, any more than it had been hard to follow the energy to the apartment, whether it made sense or not that she was compelled to follow it. Even now she was wondering just what her options were.

She sat here for a long moment, just thinking about her life, her future, wondering what she wanted to do, when Trevor opened his eyes and smiled at her.

"Did you figure it out?" he asked her.

She jumped, worried that he'd read her thoughts. The look in her gaze said it all.

"No, I don't know what you were thinking about, but it was obvious you were intent on whatever it was."

She sank back into the chair. "You shouldn't do that to people," she declared, her voice harsher than normal. "People might believe you."

"They might," he said, looking at her with interest. "And, in your case, it's really not a bad idea, is it? You have an awful lot going on in that head of yours, and, if you could just find a way to calm it, you might get somewhere."

She snorted at that. "Hey, if I could find a way to not go to random people's doors and act like an idiot, I would be totally happy."

"Yet the reason you do go there is pure. You only want to help."

She gave him a veiled look. "Whether I like it or not, it feels very much like I have to do it."

"And, therefore, don't make excuses for it. You're doing it with the best of intentions, even if it doesn't feel it's working out that way."

Just then came a knock at the door. She hopped up, but he bolted to his feet first, walked over to the door, and opened it before she had a chance. She glared at him, but he tipped the waiter and then pushed the trolley inside. The smell hit her stomach, and she groaned instead. "Wow," she murmured. "I hadn't realized how hungry I was."

"It goes along with that whole blood-sugar drop and associated temper tantrum," he said, with a chuckle.

She stared at him. "Is that what that was? A temper tantrum?"

"I don't know," he said, looking at her curiously. "Maybe that's something you should tell me."

"I don't know," she replied. "I've never acted like that before. I've never found the need to prove myself like that. It doesn't seem terribly fair, does it?"

"Maybe not fair, maybe not intentional," he stated, "but, if you think about it, it happened, and now there's this whole energy pathway." He hesitated for a moment. "Have you ever tried to follow that energy back?"

She shook her head. "Usually when I notice it, ... it's

already dispersed."

"So, if you could get a jump on it before it attacks, maybe you could figure out where it's coming from?" he asked her.

She thought about that, as she picked up a burger and stared down at the juicy goodness before her. Yet it was hard to think of food and these attacks at the same time. "Possibly," she murmured.

"But think about it. How much energy or how many people would be involved in something like this?"

"I've never really had any advance notice. I just get this nudge, and that's where I go."

He nodded. "That may be, but did you ever consider …" He hesitated, and then thought he better just come out with it. "Did you ever consider that maybe they're letting you know?"

She lifted her head, startled. "You mean, the bad guys are telling me what they're doing? No, … but then I would know ahead of time, wouldn't I?"

"But that's the question really," he said, refining that train of thought now. "Are they telling you, and you're not paying attention? Are they even talking to you? Or do you have precognition visions?" he asked. "I'm just guessing here, but, if you could track the information before it got to the point of an attack, that would be very helpful."

"Of course it would," she cried out. "Don't you think I try to do something useful with this?"

"Of course you do, and you are," he noted, giving her an understanding look. "Don't ever forget that."

"*Right.*" She rolled her eyes at him, as she took another bite. She chewed fiercely for a moment and then added, "Surely people understand that I'm not just sitting here and doing nothing, right?"

"I think so," he said, with a smile. "If anybody thought about it, they would assume you were doing something, but I don't even know what you're doing. You may not even know what you are capable of. I just know that you're finding this. So I'm wondering if you can find a way to get ahead of it."

"Maybe," she muttered, and then she looked at him with an uneasy expression. "But I'm not sure that'll make my life any easier."

"No, it may not," he agreed, with a nod, "and that's definitely part of the challenge. Yet, if you have to do whatever you can do in order to keep your sanity, yet still benefit the rest of the world, … you should take the chance."

"Why do I have to be responsible for the rest of the world?" she asked. "Why can't everybody look after themselves?" she muttered. She took another bite and chewed hard for a moment, then sighed. "Nobody else seems to know though, do they?"

"Nope," he said, with a cheeky grin in her direction. "So far, you're the only one we've found with that specific ability."

"It's not as if people like me will be sitting around at hydroelectric stations," she muttered. "That'll get you killed."

"Will it kill you though?" he asked curiously.

"I don't know," she said. "I've never tried. I really don't want to push it that far either."

"Of course not," he agreed. "As soon as you try that, … you're likely to push yourself off into the brink," he murmured, "and that is something you just can't afford."

"I sure can't. I don't want to be on a death mission here.

I just want to enjoy my life … and have it be a life that is doable and at least comfortable, if not happy.”

“Not like what we’re dealing with right now,” he noted, shaking his head. “This is terrible, as if it’s some litmus test, without any end in sight.”

They finished their meal in silence. As he cleaned up everything, he looked at her and asked, “Why don’t you have a nap?”

She shrugged. “I’m still too keyed up.”

“Then drain it. Find a spot in the floor and send all that energy right into the center of the earth,” he suggested. “You need rest before all this goes around and around in your head and stops you from doing anything, should something happen.”

At his wording, she looked over at him and raised an eyebrow. “Are you picking up on something?”

“I think we’ll have visitors soon,” he shared, “but not just yet. So I want you to get some rest and to get a little sleep at least, before then.”

Frowning, she walked over to the bed, sat down, and looked up at him. “When?”

“Not for an hour or two,” he replied, “and I’ll wake you up so you have lots of warning.”

“*Great*,” she muttered. “Are they friend or foe?”

He looked at her for a moment and shook his head. “I don’t know. That’s one of the reasons I want to ensure you’re wide awake and capable of doing whatever we need to do.”

She winced. “I don’t want to hurt anybody.”

“Good,” he said. “I wasn’t planning on it, not unless they came here to hurt us. I will deal with them, but, just in case all bets are off, then we need to do what we have to do to stay alive. So I need you to be up for anything."

It was a little hard to take in what he was saying, but she knew she needed rest. Once the food reached her stomach and the adrenaline had crashed, she dropped quickly. She curled up on the bed, pulling a blanket up over her, but not getting under the covers. "Wake me up with lots of warning."

"If there is any warning," he murmured. "Just sleep. I'll look after you."

With that, she closed her eyes and fell into a deep sleep. She didn't remember the last time she had slept quite so quickly or so heavily. Her dreams were mixed—some positive, some negative—but all had her jerking awake several times, checking that everything was okay, and then dropping back under again. When she finally surfaced the last time, she stared up at him. "No visitors?"

"Not yet," he said with a smile, as he walked over and sat down on the bed beside her. "How're you feeling?"

"Like crap. I overdid it energy-wise."

"You did," he agreed, "but it's something that we all do from time to time."

"I guess," she muttered. "Any news?"

"I did hear from Terk and Damon. The police have cleared the apartment building, and they managed to disarm the bomb, so everybody's been allowed back into their homes. Thanks to you, it didn't go off and kill anybody."

She smiled with relief. "Now that is good news to wake up to."

"Yes, but no word on who our bomb-maker is though, so he's still on the loose. Plus, it doesn't let you off the hook in terms of the cops wanting to talk to you. They will be on us, probably sooner rather than later."

"*Great.*" She rolled over, staring at the wall. "*Crazy psychic chick tells them there's a bomb in the building.* Think they'll go for that?"

"It's what it is in your mind. It doesn't matter if they go for it or not. Tell them what you know and leave it at that."

She gave a startled laugh. "That won't go over well."

He grinned. "Maybe not, but Terk is also lending some weight to this issue. Besides, you did save a lot of people with that warning," he reminded her. "So, as much as the local cops may not like it, they also have to respect the fact that it could have been much worse."

"Not something they'll want to even contemplate," she said, with a laugh. "You know they just want somebody to crucify."

"There isn't anybody they can have in this instance," he stated, his tone calm and really relaxed.

She stared at him. "Have you ever been in this situation before?"

"Several times." He nodded. "It does help if you have somebody like Terk in your corner, but, if you don't, then you tell them the truth, and you just get marked off as one of the crazies in the world."

"How sad is that," she whispered. "We do all this to help other people, and we're the ones who get marked down as being nutcases."

"True, but the alternative isn't great either."

"How so?" she asked.

"We don't want them coming to us for answers all the time when we can't provide them," he replied. "That's another aspect to this that you probably aren't seeing and likely don't want to see, but we really don't have a whole lot of answers on demand. Once the cops see that we have answers once, there's that tendency to want them all the time, … even when we don't have them. And then we get proven as charlatans."

"*Great*," she muttered.

He looked down at his watch and frowned.

"Yeah, so energy is coming toward us," she muttered, as she got up and made her way to the bathroom, where she washed her face and stepped back out again. "I just don't know if it's good or bad."

"Neither do I, but we'll find out soon enough."

When a knock came on the door a little later, he looked at her and asked, "You ready?"

She shrugged. "Sure, whatever."

He opened it to see Damon, Bullard, and two cops. Trevor looked back at her and let them in. As soon as she saw the cops, she stiffened, but, when she saw Bullard, she openly glared at him, crossing her arms over her chest. "Wow," she muttered, "this room isn't big enough for all this."

The cops looked around uneasily, and the lead cop began, "We do need to ask you some questions, if you are up to it."

"That's nice, but you could have asked me to go down to the station."

"We figured you wouldn't want to," the head cop said, looking at her cautiously.

She stared at him. "I don't have any information, nothing more than I already told you."

"I understand that, but, now that the bomb's been disarmed, … we have some questions as to how you found the information."

"Tea leaves," she stated, and that answer stopped everybody in their tracks.

Trevor gave a long-suffering sigh and added in exasperation, "She's just pissed, so don't mind her, but she is a psychic," he declared. He walked over and sat down beside her.

The police nodded. "You said that last time."

"I did, and you didn't believe me then, so you won't believe me now," she declared, with a wave of her hand. "So, what difference does it make?"

"Because, if you know anything about who did this and what the hell's going on, we need that information."

"If I had it, I would have given it to you already," she said, steadily staring at him. "They're after Bullard, but other than that, I can't tell you anything."

At that, the cops looked over at Bullard. He studied her steadily and then said in a firm voice, "We need you to come back to the compound."

She raised one eyebrow and shook her head. "That won't work out so well for me." She looked back at the cops. "You'll have to check into Bullard's life as to what's going on. I don't know who, why, or how. I just know it's connected to him."

The cop looked from Bullard back to her, then back to Bullard again. "He doesn't know what's going on."

"No? That's because he hasn't dug deep enough," she suggested. "I don't know what's going on, except it seems to be a personal matter directed at Bullard. I know that answer isn't good enough for you guys, but, beyond that, I can't help you." She looked up, saw Damon, and then something flashed. "Unless you've got any answers."

Damon shook his head. "None of us do. None of us saw this coming. None of us knew anything about it, and we had no warning except from you. That's the scary part here."

"Of course." She gave him a ghost of a smile. "Nobody wants to see shadows creeping through town or through your life, knowing that somebody's got something planned, and it's not good," she muttered, staring off into the distance. "But it happens, and it happens too often. That's what terrorist cells are all about."

"Are you saying this is a terrorist cell?" One of the cops jumped in at the mention.

She could do nothing but drop her head into her hands, silently condemning her own slip of the tongue. She raised her head with a big sigh. "No, I'm not saying that," she clarified. "I'm saying that's what terrorist cells are *like*. They operate under your nose, and you don't know anything about them until they pop up and destroy something. I was just making the comparison."

"It's an interesting analogy," one cop said. "So why would you use those particular words?"

"To help you to understand what this is about. Is it a cell? For all I know, it could be, but I don't know that it is. I also don't know that it isn't," she explained in exasperation. "This is exactly why I don't talk to cops because I don't have the answers that you're looking for. I share whatever answers come to mind, but, beyond that, I can't help you."

The cops looked stumped.

"You've obviously talked to the others, and that's why you're here, but I don't have anything more to give you," Reeni stated. "Now, if you don't mind, I need to go back to sleep." Then she shifted back into the bed, pulling the blankets up over her and glaring at the people in her room. When the cops made no move to leave, she threw back the covers. "Fine, if that is how you choose to play it, I'll just go get another room." And she brushed past them all, grabbing her purse as she headed out.

"Wait, wait, wait," Trevor said.

"No," she snapped back. "There is no waiting. I won't sit here and get persecuted."

"Nobody is persecuting you," Trevor replied in exasperation.

She turned and glared at him. "Look at them. They already think I'm guilty. I can practically hear them all thinking, and it's far too loud in my head."

"They're desperate and looking for answers," he noted. "They're not blaming you."

She stopped and turned to face the men.

Immediately they both shook their heads. "We're not. We may have come down a little hard initially because we didn't understand what was going on," the lead cop said, "but, right now, we just need all the help we can get."

She blew the strands of hair off her face. "You do need all the help you can get," she agreed, "but I don't have anything to give you. I don't like being accused. I don't like being …" She hesitated, her glance switching over to Bullard and then quickly on Trevor. "… locked up."

She huffed for a moment and then added, "Some of this is very hard for me. I don't want anybody in my space who doesn't believe in me, and you have no reason to. I started this, and I apologize for that. I probably shouldn't have had anything to do with it at all, but, … well, I was under the impression that I needed to." She was on the verge of tears, and angrily swiped at her face. "Right now, I would very much like for this to be over."

"When you say you felt as if you needed to, can you explain why?" the head cop asked.

"It felt as if it would get big and it would get ugly, and it started with Bullard," she said, staring at him. "What's so hard to understand about that?"

"That wasn't mentioned before."

"I didn't know before," she declared, with a shrug of her shoulders. "You really are asking questions that I don't have any answers for."

"We found the bombmaker's equipment."

"So surely you have some way to trace whoever was there, whoever rented the apartment, the phone numbers that they used, and where the stuff was purchased. That's what you do, right?" she asked pointedly. "And maybe that's what Bullard's guys do. I don't know. All I know is, I got messages, and I tried to enlighten people to save them from danger. And, for that, well, I can't say it's been a great event. Now, if you wouldn't mind, I'll head back to England."

At that, Trevor stiffened. "I didn't even think to ask. Where are you living these days?"

"Just outside of London," she muttered. "At least I will if I can keep away from my family."

"Why do you want to get away from your family?" one of the cops asked.

She snorted. "Because they look at me the same way you do. And that's not exactly how I want to spend my life."

The cops shared a look and frowned.

"Yeah, so if you already made some inquiries into my life, I'm sure you found out I'm just two steps free of the loony bin," she shared caustically. "That's another reason I don't want to hang around with you."

"Wait, wait, wait," one of the cops said in exasperation. "Look. We obviously had to do an investigation into who you are."

"You don't know anything about who I am," she declared, her voice rising, as Trevor felt the hysteria also rising below the surface. "Nothing that your computer spits out says anything about who I really am. I don't even begin to try and explain it anymore, but what I can tell you right now is, … I simply don't have any more information."

"Yet you just gave them something," Trevor pointed out in a calm, collected, and soothing tone.

She glared at him. "I didn't give them anything because I don't know what I have in my head. If they ask questions, and I have an answer, I can give it. Yet, if they're asking me to just spit out information, as if I'm some printer run amok, I don't have it," she snapped, glaring at him.

"That's not a bad thing. Maybe just have a seat and try to calm down. We'll bring in some fresh coffee, and let's see if they ask any questions that might stir up some more information."

She hesitated, and the cops stepped forward, nodding. "Please," they said together. The older one added, "We really would appreciate it."

"But you don't even believe in psychics," she stated pointedly. "I can tell from your energy, so why would I want to put myself through this?"

"We don't believe because we've never had any exposure," the other one offered. "So, we get it. We're not the typical go-round, but you're not our typical go-round either," he said in an understanding tone. She could see his confusion, but while there may have been doubt, there was no deception. "We're just trying to find information. If we pool our resources, maybe we can get there."

She walked back to fling herself down onto the chair. "Yeah, it'll take more than coffee."

Trevor snorted and quickly picked up the room service

phone and called in an order for six coffees and rounds of dessert. She perked up at that. He nodded. "You're worse than I am," Trevor noted. "The way to your heart is definitely through your stomach."

"Yeah, my heart is pretty-well locked up."

Shaking his head, he smiled. "Your heart is an open book."

She glared at him and soon turned away, only to be facing the men who were now staring at her with interest. She shrugged. "He doesn't know me as well as he thinks he does."

"Nobody knows us as well as we think we do," Bullard interjected, as he stared at her uncomfortably. "When we meet some people, it can trigger reactions we didn't think we had in us, like I triggered in you."

"And I triggered in you," she replied.

He flushed at that. "Touché, both of us apparently hit some sparks off each other."

She shrugged. "That's fine. Every time you look at your gate, you'll remember me, I'm sure of it."

He rolled his eyes at that. "Yeah, thanks for blowing it up."

At that, the cops stiffened and turned to him. "Just kidding," he said, with a smile and a shrug. "I didn't mean it that way." They seemed to relax slightly at that.

Then Reeni laughed, and the moment passed. "Maybe that's what I needed, a laugh at Bullard's expense." Then she looked over at the cops and added, "Start asking your questions. I feel I am up for it, at least for a while."

And that began what felt like a trip from hell, right down a lava slide.

Did she have any idea who lived in the apartment?

Did she have any idea who bought the materials?

Did she have any idea who the targets were?

Did she have any idea if it was connected to anybody else in the building?

The questions kept coming, fast and furious, and her answers were equally fast. *Yes, no, yes, yes, no, no, no.* Then she gave a couple names and shrugged. "I don't think the names have anything to do with this, but they're there." Then she frowned. "No, wait, there's one name that does matter. *Josiah.* I don't have a last name for you though, and I feel as if he's dead. But somehow or other he's a part of this." She turned and looked at Bullard, then narrowed her gaze. "You are a part of it, so who is Josiah to you?"

He shook his head. "I have no idea."

"You need to figure it out then," she stated, "because he is the reason for this in some way, and that's how you are connected."

On a long exhale, Bullard replied, "I don't know that name."

"You don't know that name because you knew him by another name, but he died." She pondered that. "I … I'm getting that it was about three to four years ago, and it involved some job you did." She looked at Bullard and gave him a smirk. "You have a lot of enemies."

He nodded noncommittally, then shrugged. "Yeah, when you do a lot of work for governments around the world, trying to keep people safe and putting criminals behind bars, you wind up with enemies."

She didn't say anything to that because she knew he was correct, though it didn't make things any easier. Still, she did feel the need to add one thing. "I know that it's connected to you, and you'll need to go back in time." She pondered that, frowning as she tried to concentrate. "I'm still getting three to four years ago."

Just then the coffee arrived. Reeni got up and poured herself a cup, then begrudgingly poured one for everyone else as well, realizing that, as long as everybody was cooperative, she might get out of this with a simple end to the questioning. She didn't know. Then she had a horrible thought. She looked over at the cops. "Did you contact my family?"

One of them flushed and nodded.

"*Great*," she muttered, rolling her shoulders up and down, as if to ease the instant tension that flooded her body at the very thought of her family. "Did they say anything?"

"Your father mentioned something about coming over to see you."

She swallowed hard and stared at him. Then she looked around the room, breathing too hard. "That's guaranteed to move me along. I need to get away from here right now. I presume you told him where I am?"

They nodded, bewildered.

"*Right*." She started packing up her belongings. "Thanks for nothing."

"He's your father, with—"

"Yeah, he's my father, but, if you think he's got my best interests at heart, you're wrong," she snapped, tears already burning her eyes. Just when she thought she could calm down and relax, that had to come up.

As she was still packing up, Bullard stepped inside and she realized something had shifted. "What's going on?"

"Apparently we weren't supposed to let her father know where she was," one of the cops shared. "We contacted family as part of our initial inquiry, not realizing it was a problem for her."

"Ah." Bullard winced. "Come back to the compound with us."

"No," she snapped. "I'm not going there. I'll just disappear again."

"You can't keep running," he said.

"Oh, you might be surprised."

"Why would you run?" the one cop asked, increasingly bewildered.

"Because my father doesn't care about me. He cares about making sure I'm not an embarrassment to him," she explained. "So, by telling him where I am, and possibly all the loony answers I gave you for being here, you've given him the ammunition to come over with a slew of his lawyers and doctors to try to put me behind bars again."

"In jail?" he asked.

"It might as well be jail." She glared at him. "He wants to keep me confined in a mental hospital so I can't embarrass him any longer." The cops looked uncomfortable, as they glanced from one to the other. "You can think I'm crazy all you want," she snapped, as she walked into the bathroom and brought out her toiletries. "That's your headache, but I'm leaving, and I really don't give a crap what you do."

And, with that, she stormed out of the hotel room and slammed the door hard.

TREVOR BOLTED OUT the door behind her. He didn't even bother saying a word to the men left behind, still stunned and staring at the door. He caught up with her at the bottom of the stairs, as she'd taken the elevator. As soon as the doors opened, and she took a step out, saw him, and glared, then retreated back inside the elevator.

He stood there, watching her expression, one of desperation. "What will you do, Reeni? I'm not here to imprison you. I'm not here to hurt you. I only want to help."

"Help?" she repeated, staring at him. "There is no help. I need to go into hiding. My father is nothing if not determined to get rid of the blot on his name."

He winced at that. "Then I'll help you do that too."

"Oh, and how will you do that?" she asked, with a sneer. "He scares everybody off, remember?"

"I don't scare that easily," he said in exasperation. "Plus, certain people lend credence to our abilities."

She hesitantly stepped out of the elevator, as other people crowded in. With her bag over her shoulder, she walked out to the front of the hotel, then looked over at him and shook her head. "No way Terk will want help now. Taking me in is one thing, but getting involved with my father is just bad news."

"Your father is not all that powerful," Trevor declared. "And a lot of other people are in this world who appreciate what you do."

"Not very many," she murmured. "Apparently I don't have any people skills."

"Your people skills could definitely use a brush-up," he suggested, with a gentle smile. "Yet I think you're wrong. I think plenty of people like you very much."

"Bullshit," she snapped. "You only have to look at how Bullard treated me."

Trevor hesitated. "It seems Bullard's feelings are pretty rough over it all as it is, but the fact is, he's not the one who brought your father in."

"No, it was those do-gooder morons at the police department."

"In fairness, that's what they do. It's standard practice to check in with the families, when it comes to something like this."

"Yeah? Because families are supposed to be supportive and helpful, but, in my case, contacting them is the worst thing anyone could possibly do." As she headed outside, a huge limo pulled up in front of them. She ducked behind a balustrade and raced around the corner of the building. Crouching now, she watched her father get out of the limo, irritation evident in every line of his body as he strode forward, his men and his assistant racing to catch up with him. They were talking a mile a minute about their plans as soon as he dealt with this.

This being her.

Trevor shook his head, knowing it wasn't the time to brace the man, and headed around the corner behind her. As he got there, he swore because he saw no sign of her. That wasn't cool. He turned, searching the entire area for her, and, when he couldn't find her, he pulled out his phone and called her.

Things got worse yet when she didn't answer.

"Well, damn," he muttered.

He closed his eyes, knowing her energy well, and just started to follow it. He had to open his eyes several times to realign himself. By the time he made a few turns, he found her up ahead, striding at a pace that was hard to keep up with. Afraid of losing her, he ran and caught up with her. "Nice try."

She looked at him, then shrugged. "I wasn't trying to do anything, but that was my father, so I just left."

"I needed to confirm it was him."

"I didn't need that," she declared, with a hard laugh. "I knew it was him the minute I saw the car. That's the way he travels, always."

"Right now, he'll probably be a bit delayed, while the police have a talk with him."

"That'll be fun for them too." She snickered. "I'm almost sorry I left early. I might have enjoyed the fireworks."

"Yet there wouldn't be fireworks if you hadn't left," he pointed out.

"Yeah, that's true. Everybody just falls in line and does what Dad says. I thought that maybe being over here would be different, but apparently he has pull everywhere."

"Once the cops called him, I'm sure he grabbed the first flight he could get and headed over."

She looked at him sideways. "Grabbed a flight? He has his own plane, remember?"

"Right," he muttered, shaking his head, forgetting how the uber-rich lived. "Do you really think you'll hide from him?"

"I've managed to for the last few years, but, every once in a while, he catches up with me. Then I have to escape again."

"Are we talking about the need to escape now?" he asked.

"Yes," she snapped, frowning at him. "I get that, for you guys, this is just over-the-top BS, but, for me, who has no tools and no support, trying to fight him off and to get away from him isn't fun," she explained, "particularly when he has all the resources, and somehow cancels my credit cards and seizes my bank accounts."

Trevor frowned. "Without your permission?"

"Absolutely," she muttered.

"You think that's legal?"

"No, it sure as hell isn't, but it's not as if I can fight him myself, and it's not as if anybody will help me fight him."

At that, Trevor's own temper rippled through him. "Are these bank accounts that you opened on your own?"

"Absolutely, but he somehow managed to get power of attorney over me, and that is how he manages to make my life miserable. All of that began when I was still a child, so he had complete parental control. He had power of attorney over my sister too, until she agreed to marry who he wanted her to."

"But that's archaic," he muttered.

"Yeah, well, that's my father," she stated, "and he's just gotten worse. Now that my sister has dutifully produced twin boys, she is essentially the golden girl again—or still, I guess," she shared, with a hard laugh. "Maybe she's happy. I hope she's happy, but I don't know that she really knows what happiness is. Arranged marriages produce that series of babies, and maybe that was her condition for getting free. I don't know. But the reality is, dear old Dad is not to be trusted when it comes down to it anyway," she grumbled. "I'll just get caught up in all that nonsense of his again, but the reality is that I'm even more unprotected here."

"In what way?"

"I don't have anybody here to help me," she said, facing him now. "It's not exactly a country that you want to be left stranded in."

"Right, but that won't happen, not while I'm here."

She laughed. "You came to help Bullard, so you need to do that."

"Maybe so, but I also came to help you, and I'll do that as well. Not to mention the fact that, besides all that, Bullard still owes you one."

"I don't give a crap what Bullard thinks. I don't want anything to do with him."

Trevor hesitated. "I don't think that's fair to Bullard."

"I don't give a crap about that either," she declared. "You seem to think that he owes me something, but I don't, and I'm not sticking around where I'm not wanted. I sure as hell won't give him a second chance to play patriarch and to threaten to imprison me again. For all I know, he's the one who contacted my father."

"He wouldn't do that," Trevor said, "and the police already told you that it was them. So you're really not being fair. Honestly, Bullard would be one of your best bets for fighting your father, not to mention Terk, plus Levi for that matter."

She shrugged. "I've already tried to get help, and, in the end, everybody always ends up buckling under dear old Dad's threats."

"Sounds like a challenge to me, and I can guarantee they would be all in on a *dear old dad needs to be put in his place* mission."

"Yeah, well, that ain't happening." She snorted.

"What about your mom?'

"What about her?" she asked, shaking her head at him. "She produced two daughters, no sons, and then lost the ability to reproduce. For all I know, half-a-dozen illegitimate ones are out there in his attempt to secure more male heirs. I know my mother was always a disappointment to him when she couldn't give him the sons he needed."

"Even though it's the father who determines the gender of the baby via either an X or Y chromosome?"

"Yeah, well, my father is never one to let the facts get in

the way. And honestly, if he could do a test-tube baby—and for all I know he has—it's not as if I've been around much for the last several years. But, if there's a chance at having a male heir somewhere along the line, believe me that Dad wouldn't have hesitated to get a surrogate to carry it."

"Maybe he did," Trevor acknowledged. "How would you feel about that?"

"Grateful, unless it'll be yet another heavy-handed male trying to determine what my life should be," she snapped.

"Okay, so do you have a plan right now?" he asked, considering they were still storming down the main street, but one block over where not so much traffic converged.

"I'll find a place to hole up in for a while. I'll need some sleep and some food, but more than that I need safety, and safety when my father is around … just doesn't happen."

Trevor could see just how traumatized she was by the arrival of her father, and he felt awful for her. It didn't make sense that her father had such a long reach, and that was also bothering him. He needed somebody to step up and to give him a hand in terms of what the father could and could not do legally, plus how to get all those controls away from him because that was the next issue. As long as he had any legal power over Reeni, then her life would always be like this. He pointed to a small place up ahead. "Let's go in there."

She looked at it and shrugged. "I don't know why you think that place is any better than another."

"The energy seems easier."

She contemplated that for a moment and nodded. "Fine, but nobody says I'm staying."

That reply half explained the prickly personality that he was seeing way more of than he had expected. She hid it well, until something went wrong, and then it all blew up, which was what happened when Bullard threatened to keep her on his premises. He'd set off a firestorm that nobody had been prepared for. "What if the cops still want to talk to you?" Trevor asked her.

"I'll probably end up stealing a car and driving out of the country, so I hope I can get a long way away from here before anybody can stop me," she muttered. He sucked in his breath, and she glared at him. "If you think I'm staying around to let my father be the same controlling asshole I know he is, you're wrong."

"I get that, and I can see that he really terrifies you, but there has to be some way to get your freedom."

"I don't think that's even possible because he doesn't hand over control well. Hell, he just doesn't want to hand over control *period*."

"Do you have any contact with your sister?"

She shook her head. "No, I sure don't, not since she dutifully married the man our father chose for her."

"Did she tell you that she didn't want to get married?"

"Yeah, she did. She bawled the whole day before her wedding. It was one of those huge, over-the-top, half-million-dollar type weddings," she told him. "And all she could do was bawl because she couldn't stand who she was marrying. After that, she popped out two kids in quick succession. Maybe she's been carted off to a mental institution by now. She wouldn't talk to me back then, so it's not likely she'll talk to me now. I'm pretty damn sure that she doesn't give a crap anymore, as long as she's done her job in Dad's eyes. Maybe that will get her free from her husband's unwanted attentions, or who knows? Maybe she's fallen in love with him. I have no way of knowing."

It was such a foreign concept to Trevor that he didn't

really know how to respond, since this was out of the Dark Ages, in his opinion. What bothered him more than anything was Reeni literally running away, one step away from a flat-out sprint, as she sought a place to hide. It was all he could do to keep up with her. When he finally managed to get her inside the one hotel he'd picked out, she stopped at the registration desk and asked how much it was for a room. When she heard the amount, she just nodded, pulled cash out of her pocket, and paid.

He wanted to step in, but she wouldn't even let him get close. He realized once again that it was all about control. If she paid, then she felt as if she could pick up and leave as soon as she needed to. The fact that she automatically assumed she would need to wounded him in a way that he had no idea he could even be hurt. He was alternately cursing Bullard, cursing her father, and cursing life in general when she turned and glared at him.

"Fine, I have a place to stay now. So you can go away."

He snorted. "Yeah, that's not happening."

She fisted her hands on her hips in the elevator, as they went up to the room that she'd been given on the sixth floor. "Maybe you just need to go off and get a life, instead of trying to play Sir Galahad," she snapped, with a half laugh, but absolutely no humor was in it.

He shook his head. "No. I have to think about this. I'm not sure what the best plan of action is at the moment," he shared, "but it won't involve your going back into a mental hospital."

"Yeah, well, unless you can make miracles in your world, absolutely no way you'll stop it. I'm the one who's very aware of what I have to do, and I will do it. So don't expect me to stick around if things get ugly."

"I can understand that," he agreed, "but you can't run forever."

She stared at him and asked, "Wanna bet?" And, with that, she turned and headed into the bathroom and slammed the door in his face.

CHAPTER 7

REENI SAT DOWN on the toilet with the seat closed and buried her head in her hands. She wanted to bawl but she didn't want Trevor to hear her. She didn't want him out there at all. If he wasn't here, she could do what she really wanted to do—curl up into a tiny ball and hide the fear that had hit her as soon as she found out her father had been informed of her location. That had changed everything. She didn't even know how to leave the country now.

She had her paperwork. She had everything she needed, but her father was cagey, and he could quite possibly stop her from getting onto a plane. She needed to get a vehicle somehow and to drive like hell. Even at that, she stared down at her hands and watched as the shaking took over. How was she supposed to do this?

He shouldn't have been here at all, and he shouldn't have any idea that she was here either. Yet, due to the police, due to her attempt to help, *this* happened. Once the tears started, she couldn't stop them. They just poured and poured. So she sat here, not sure how to handle it, desperately trying to quiet her crying so Trevor wouldn't hear. When the door opened, she heard his muffled exclamation, and she was quickly picked up and carried out to the other room. When she was settled into his lap on the couch, he just held her.

She cried and cried and cried. She didn't know whether it was just the stress of everything piling on together or something else, but she needed the release. By the time she finally ran down and went quiet in his arms, she didn't have anything to say. She just let the last of the tears roll down her cheeks, as she contemplated having to make a run for it again. She thought that maybe Trevor would help her, but she didn't want to put him in her father's sights.

When she finally stopped crying, he just held her close, his hand gently rubbing her shoulders.

She whispered, "I'm sorry."

"Don't ever be sorry for that," he said. "I'm just sorry your father brings out such an instant panic."

She nodded. "Me too. No matter how much I try to deal with it, the minute I see him and hear him, … it just sets me off."

"Of course it does. Why wouldn't it? As long as he has paperwork to control what you do and how you do it, you'll never have the freedom to do whatever you want with your life."

She shook her head and leaned back slightly to look up at him. "I know. My grandmother didn't like anything about the way my father handled me. I'm pretty sure she had the sight as well," Reeni shared. "So she left me enough money that I'll be okay for a long time."

"Do you think your father's after that too?"

She stared at him and then shrugged. "I guess when they say, *the rich can never be rich enough*, it's possible, but I think it's more about power. I think it's also about not damaging his name, not doing anything to tarnish his reputation, whatever that means in this world." She snorted. "It's all just so damn sad, yet, because of who he is and what he's done, I don't really have the ability to fight him. I can't ever get tested independently, and no one will ever buck him."

"Because he has so much money?"

"I think he's harsh to deal with in many ways," she added. "I don't even know if he's on the up-and-up in business. I just know that he's ruthless when it comes to me." Trevor didn't say anything. "You know you're better off just letting me go, right?"

He laughed. "Yeah, I'm not very good at that. And the more I hold you, the more I realize I don't really want to let you go at all."

She shook her head. "And that'll just take you down a pathway with absolutely no joy. My future is determined by him, and I don't have any way to go against that."

He pondered that, just holding her in his arms. "Not everybody is afraid of your father."

"Everybody I know is," she declared. "Nobody in my world is willing to buck him. I tried hard. I really did, but even my own grandmother couldn't fight him, and that just made her really sad. When she passed, she left me a letter, telling me that I needed to find somebody somewhere to help me get out from under his control. I haven't been able to do it, so I just keep running, trying to stay ahead of him and his long-arm reach, even here. I'm in Africa, for God's sake," she muttered, and her eyes had a sheen of tears again. "I thought for sure I would be safe here."

"So, his home base is America?"

"Texas," she clarified, "where everything's bigger, badder, and better, as far as he's concerned."

Trevor just nodded and didn't say anything.

She nestled against his arms, realizing that it was the first time she'd had anybody she could confide in. "It feels so strange to even tell you," she murmured.

"That's because you've been keeping it all bottled up this whole time. And that's on top of the fact that we have bombers out there and somebody's targeting Bullard."

She nodded. "Yet Bullard isn't anybody I want to deal with either."

"But that's the thing, Bullard has a lot of influence," he noted. "He's a guy who could do something for you."

She laughed. "He might if he wanted to, but he won't want to. Even if he did, there would be a price to pay, and it's probably something I couldn't pay anyway," she grumbled. "Everybody wants something. Regardless, what Bullard could do, even in this country, won't clear me anywhere else."

"Maybe not, but that doesn't mean Terk couldn't help out."

She stared at him. "What could Terk even do, and why would he do anything?"

"If you worked with him—hell, even if you didn't, just being an energy worker makes you eligible—you would be under that umbrella, which includes Levi's team in the US, Texas no less, and Bullard's here in Africa. You would have powerful help on three continents that have worldwide reaches as well."

"I think you put way too much stock in that umbrella of Terk's," she muttered. "He would need one hell of a lot of pull with all those governments to make that happen."

He looked at her with surprise and then grinned. "Sweetheart, he has a hell of a lot of pull with a lot of governments, the US included. Last I checked, he is best buds with MI6 these days too."

She frowned at that. "But so does my father. He has a lot

of pull in a lot of places."

"With governments or just with business?"

"Business for sure," she said. "I don't know about governments, but, if he can bribe them, he will." At that he stiffened beneath her, and she frowned. "Isn't that how business is done?" she asked in a mocking tone.

"Do you know of anybody he's bribed?"

She pondered that and then shrugged. "I have a few names. I know he's done some pretty shitty deals in the past, but I don't think he's done anything criminal, like murdering anyone," she noted. "And that's unfortunate in a way because, boy, if I could bring down that house of cards, I would be more than happy to."

He didn't reply right away, and she knew that nobody could really do anything to help.

"Let me talk to Terk about it."

"Yeah? No time to talk. I'll stay here while I figure out what my next move is, and then go from there," she said.

"What would be your next move ideally?" he asked. "I mean, where will you go?"

"If I can find out where he is and stay one step ahead of him, he'll get tired eventually. He'll probably leave a keeper behind, somebody to continue to look for me, but he'll be pissed that he was disturbed enough to personally come over here."

"God, I just love your father," he muttered.

"Nobody does, that's the thing. He's got a lot of enemies, but it's that way on a personal level too, just because he—" She ran out of words, shrugged. "He is who he is. Growing up with him was brutal, but, once my abilities started to develop, he became a threat in ways that I couldn't even begin to imagine. That made my life very difficult and him very dangerous for me."

"I get that, but we can come up with some answers," Trevor offered. "I won't let this happen to you anymore."

"It's too late," she declared, staring at him. "He's here. Whether I can stay ahead of him or not, I don't know, but he's here, and he won't go away on a permanent basis. He's been looking for me for too long to just give up now."

"How long?"

She winced. "It's been four years this time."

"Well, hell." He grinned at her in admiration. "Good for you."

She laughed. "Sure, but then again I have a different name on my passport, so that helps. That was something my grandmother set up before she passed away."

"Wow, I really like your grandmother, but seriously, you travel under a different name?"

"Sure." She chuckled. "So far, I haven't had anybody question it. I have IDs to go with it, so that's what I show. Once she got me the passport, which apparently she got from some shady dealer for an awful lot of money, it's made my life a whole lot easier. I think she did it because of what my father did to her, and she didn't want him to do the same to me."

"Did he hurt her?" he asked, staring at her.

"I don't think so, but she was kept isolated at the end of her life. I'm not sure she ever had any visitors or anything. She had all the best care, of course," she added in a mocking tone, "but she lived completely alone in one room where he controlled everything."

"Was it his mother or his stepmother?"

"His biological mother, and I think that's one of the reasons why he did what he did and why she did what she did. She knew what he was like, inside and out. Plus, he knew what she would have done if she'd had the chance. He never could figure out how I was traveling, and that'll be my biggest problem if I lose that," she admitted, "I'm … I'm done for then, and I might as well just walk in there and surrender."

"What would he do?"

"Fly me back home again, probably lock me up in an institution, arrange for more of his special *testing*," she replied, emphasizing the word with air quotes. "Of course that would say, once again, that I'm most definitely not capable of being out in the world on my own, then *boom*. Just like that, he controls my inheritance and everything else."

"Yet, if he has power of attorney over you, can't he do that now?"

"Except not with my grandmother's money. She set that up privately, so it's under a different name, and he has no idea what that name is."

"Now I really like your grandmother. I may love her," he said, with a grin.

She smiled, tears in her eyes. "I loved her too. She's the only one who really ever got me, the only one who understood just what my life was like with my father."

"Probably because she knew herself."

"I think so, and I think she knew better than I did, certainly earlier than I did, and yet keeping quiet had definitely taken its toll. As Dad got older, he got uglier and more powerful, more driven by power. I think seeing what was happening to me caused my grandmother to start making plans on her own."

"That shows an awful lot of love and care that we don't

always see from family members. You got lucky there. She realized what you were up against and did an awful lot to keep you safe during these years with that money, the passport, and ID."

She nodded. "That's part of the problem, and something I'm acutely aware of. Without that, I don't have anything," she said, tearing up again. "So, if he can ever figure out how I'm doing this and what name I'm traveling under, you can bet he'll put a stop to it."

"So, we have to do something about it quickly, before he finds out."

When a knock came on the door, she buried her fist into her mouth, holding back her scream. He gave her a reassuring hug and whispered, "It's just Damon."

She stared at him wide-eyed, as he hopped up, opened the door, and let Damon in. As soon as the door closed behind him, Damon looked at her. "How are you?"

She just shrugged and didn't say anything. She knew the tear tracks on her face would be hard to hide anyway, so no point in trying to avoid the obvious. The truth was, she was still panicked. but at least it had gotten down to a level where she could almost think again. "Did anybody see my father?" The fear was evident in her tone.

"He's at the hotel, raising complete hell, and the police are all over it, trying to figure out a way to handle him. Meanwhile Bullard is raising no small amount of hell on his own," he shared, with a satisfied smile. "It seems he has found the right way to let out all his bottled-up energy."

She winced at that. "I'm sure that's fun to watch."

"I don't think *fun* is the right word, but Bullard's definitely on your side," he stated, "so don't you ever doubt that."

She stared at him. "What? Why would he be on my side, when he already made it abundantly clear what he thought of me?"

"No, he had a lapse in judgment. He reacted out of frustration, fury, and fear for his own family," Damon explained. "Keep that in mind too."

She frowned, not willing to let Bullard off the hook so easily.

"Bullard would like you to come back to his place."

She shook her head. "Nope, not happening."

Damon sighed. "It's the safest place for you."

"It's a prison," she snapped, "and he made that very clear the last time I was there. So the answer is no. I can't run if Dad has any way to stop me from running, like my father paying Bullard enough money to keep me prisoner."

At that, Damon's eyebrows shot up. "Bullard won't bite, but is your father likely to do that crap?"

Just then energy slammed into her, and she shuddered, bending over, her head between her knees.

"Easy, easy, easy," Trevor muttered, as he sat down beside her again. "What was that?"

She gasped. "Something, something to do with Bullard. No, not Bullard, Bullard's place." She stared at him in shock, then bolted to her feet. "I don't know what it is, but it's major."

Damon already had his phone out, making a call. He talked to someone quickly, then turned to her and nodded. "A bomb just went off at the front door."

She nodded. "Yeah, and a second one is in the compound."

He stared at her. "Do you know where?"

"No, I don't know where, at least not from here, but it's

electrical again. Our bad guy's using some electrical device to set it off."

"Bullard's on his way there, so, if he's not already there by now, believe me that his team's on it."

"Yeah, his team's on it, but—" She frowned, looking far off into the distance. "There's something odd about it."

"Something odd?"

"Yeah, something odd," she snapped. "But, if you're asking me what, I can't tell you, not from here."

"Then that's the answer," Damon declared. "Let's go." As she sank onto the couch, Damon frowned. "You're really that scared of going back to Bullard's place?"

She bit her bottom lip and looked over at Trevor.

Trevor explained, "She spent a lot of years locked up in a sanatorium because of her father, and whatever Bullard said to her triggered the same unpleasant memories and power-control fights," he murmured. "So, yeah, she's definitely that worried."

Damon crouched in front of her. "Look. I promise that I will personally ensure you can leave any time you want to leave."

She shook her head. "You can't go up against him."

"Bullard? Or your dad?"

"Both."

"Absolutely I can. I've been friends with Bullard for a long time," he added.

"So, that just means you'll take his side. And my father will just bribe you or threaten you to join his side."

"There is no side," Damon declared. "And I can't be bought or threatened. We stand up to asshole bullies. Plus, when Bullard's wrong, he knows how to make it up to someone," he shared. "And it does happen. We all make mistakes. We all get triggered, particularly when our own family is being threatened—which isn't something Bullard's really had to deal with before. I wouldn't react that way under any other circumstance. I can understand his saying something like that, but I don't think he meant it, at least not the way that you took it."

"There is only one way to take that," she snapped, staring at him.

"Given what you've been through, yes. For you, that makes sense, but not for everybody else."

"What is it you want me to do?" she asked cautiously.

"I want you to help us find the second bomb."

"They should be able to find it without me," she replied. "They have detectors for bugs and things. Right? I mean—"

"You tell me. Will that cut it?" Damon asked her, his phone out again.

"Yes, and he should check the north quarter of the property. Somewhere around … a big power box, maybe on the street side. Something is wrong with it."

He smiled. "I really love your *something's wrong with it* description."

She shrugged. "If I knew anything more about it, maybe I could help, but I don't," she stated, "and that doesn't appear to be something my mind wraps around very easily. I just see the power and the electrical currents, but I don't see the hardware."

"Good enough," Damon noted, with a cheerful tone. He stepped back and made a phone call, then turned and looked at her. "They all want to see you back there."

"Sure, they do," she muttered, with a shrug. "But why would I walk into a place wired for bombs?" He stared at her, and she sighed. "Fine, but, if anything bad happens"—

she glared at Damon—"I won't be responsible for what I do."

At that, he stared at her for a long moment, as if contemplating the gate that she had exploded already. Then he nodded. "That's fair, and everybody is aware of that, and we'll do our best to ensure it's as peaceful as possible."

She frowned. "If Bullard's returning, it won't be peaceful. He doesn't know the meaning of the word."

He grinned at her. "Oh, he does. He's just a little bit like a bull in a china shop, that's all. He's used to getting his way."

"And that's my father," she snapped.

"Except Bullard doesn't hurt people."

"Sure he does, if it's warranted."

He sighed, then nodded. "Okay, so you got me there. If it's warranted, yes, he does, and, if it means keeping his family safe, yes, he will. With the jobs that we do, the nature of our work," he shared, "unfortunately it's what we have to do. Sometimes it's easy. Sometimes it's not. Sometimes it works, and sometimes it doesn't." He added, "The bottom line is, this is the world we live in, and, just like he's trying to protect his family, you need somebody to help protect you."

She laughed bitterly. "There's never been anybody to do that since my grandmother died."

He looked from her over to Trevor, who quickly explained what her grandmother had done. Damon's eyebrows shot up, and he whistled. "Man, I wish we all had grandparents like her."

Trevor nodded. "Yeah, me too."

"I wish I could have done something to help her toward the end of her life, but I couldn't," Reeni admitted. "She suffered for what she did for me. ... She sent me a letter, smuggled it out privately through a nurse. It probably cost her one thousand dollars to get that damn letter out," she muttered. "She warned me that my father was determined to control me, more determined than ever, and that I needed to get the hell out of there. So, once I escaped, that was it. I was done and gone, and I haven't been back since. He found me about four years ago, but I managed to escape again, and that was it. He hasn't seen me since."

"He has paperwork?" Damon asked.

"Yes, but then he had that paperwork made well before I was an adult, and I didn't have any standing in the matter," she explained. "But I can't fight it because good luck if anybody has that mental-health paperwork against you. Even if I did get a chance to fight it, he's got money, and he's got power, and he's threatening, and he doesn't hesitate to use all that."

"That's a bad deal," Damon agreed, "but there are ways. We'll look into it. You helped sort out Bullard's mess, and we'll help you navigate this one."

She frowned at him.

Trevor watched her closely. "It's a good deal. … As I mentioned earlier, between Terk and Levi and Bullard, they have an awful lot of connections, and an awful lot of abilities."

"Abilities, yeah. Abilities that didn't get you guys locked up. You don't know what it's like."

"Maybe not that part," Damon agreed, "but it did get us targeted by our own government."

She winced. "And here I thought you guys had pull with the government. I don't need *that* kind of pull," she declared, staring at him. "I've got my own damn father after me, so I sure don't need the government on my ass too."

At that, Damon chuckled. "I hear you there." He gave her a wide grin. "That's not the kind of pull we have, yet just surviving that attack on us, we do have extra leverage when we need it. We will use it when we have to," he pointed out. "This seems to be one of those times that we might need it."

"But you can't say that," she declared, frowning at him. "You aren't Terk—or Levi or Bullard."

"No, I'm not, but Terk would know what our odds are when it comes to getting this resolved," he stated. "So why don't we put a little bit of faith into the process, just like people put some faith in you and what you can do. And we'll all go from there." And he stepped forward and held out his hand to help her up.

She hesitated, looked up at Trevor, and frowned.

Trevor smiled at her, then turned to Damon. "The thing about her is, if you give her a choice, she'll always say no." So Trevor walked over, grabbed her hand, and gently lifted her to her feet. "Damon's just trying to help you," Trevor said. "And, right now, help is what you need. Let somebody help you for a change."

She nodded. "I do need help, but you guys make me very nervous sometimes."

"Only sometimes?" Damon asked.

She sighed. "Fine. I'll go help Bullard, but, if he says one more thing to me about holding me there, I'm out of there."

"He's likely to say a lot of things, and any one of them could set you off, depending on how you interpret them," Damon explained. "But, aside from those verbal slipups, we won't let anything bad happen to you. Bullard won't let anything bad happen to you."

She shuddered. "You don't give me a whole lot of choice, and I'm out of options right now. If I did have a choice, believe me that I wouldn't be here, and that you guys would never find me."

"I don't know about that." Damon smirked. "I'm pretty sure Trevor has got your number."

She groaned and turned to Trevor. "How the hell is it you even knew how to find me here?"

"I followed your energy," he said. "And, yes, if you were to run to ground and hide away on me, I could do it again. So why don't we just stop that whole *running away* thing and see if we can find a solution that's a bit more permanent?"

"That's what I really want more than anything. I want to sleep at night and to not be afraid of waking up with my father standing over my head, threatening to lock me back up again," she admitted. "If you can find a way to make that happen, that would be amazing."

He wrapped an arm around her shoulders and nodded. "I will. Now come on. Let's go deal with one issue at a time."

"If my father sees you helping me, it will make you a target as well," she warned.

"Oh, I wasn't planning on letting your father see us." He turned to Damon. "Can you run camouflage?"

"I can long enough to get you both to the compound, yep."

He seemed confident and secure in his element, and that was enough for Reeni.

Damon pointed to the door. "Let's go then. Once we're at Bullard's place, your father can't touch you."

"Yeah, *he* might not, but someone is already trying." At that, both men stiffened, and she shrugged. "They're not in yet, but they're trying. I can feel the intruder's electrical current coursing through the system. Bullard's people have no internet, no phones, no lights. Nothing's working, so your team is working blind." she explained. "If you want to save them, we need to get there fast."

TREVOR LED THE way back outside, Damon already cloaking them. Then Damon took over, hotwiring a car for their use. They kept a wary eye on their surroundings, just in case her father popped up. Even cloaked, if the limo ran into their cloaked vehicle, that was a dead giveaway. That was a complication they really couldn't afford right now, not when they had a more urgent need to deal with finding a bomb at Bullard's compound. As they quickly hopped into the vehicle, Damon drove them toward Bullard's.

Trevor's phone rang. *Bullard.* Trevor put it on Speakerphone and told Bullard, "We're on the way, and, yes, she's with us, but it was a hard decision for her to agree. However, according to her, somebody's cut your power and is trying to get into the compound and has a second bomb in place, so ensure everybody's on full alert. She mentioned the power box outside on the street. Do you have one out there?"

When Bullard replied on the other end, Trevor turned and nodded at her. "Get the city to shut it down. Reeni says there's a problem with it. I can't tell you what the problem is, but there's a problem." That ended the call. He asked her, "Are you doing okay?"

She shrugged. "I'm fine."

Yet he watched her wrap her arms around herself, hugging herself tightly. He smiled. "You'll be fine." She didn't say anything, and he knew that trust was a really big thing for her right now. He wanted to beat the hell out of her asshole of a father for having put her in this position time and time again. At that thought, he sent a text off to Terk, bringing him up to speed. Terk sent back a thumbs-up, adding they would include Levi into the loop, all looking into it further.

Trevor didn't know what that meant, but, if anybody could look into this shit, it would be Terk first and foremost. Also Trevor remembered how Ice's father was a doctor in California and had his own clinic. So maybe Levi could use those connections to at least get information on how to stop this institutionalization of Reeni. Trevor could see why in some cases that it would be necessary, yet the potential for abuse of such processes gave him pause.

Reeni's father didn't seem to be the least bit concerned about finding out if his daughter was truly of sound mind. Trevor winced. Anybody else's father might be misguided, believing he was doing the best thing possible for his child. However, Trevor knew Reeni's father to be power-mad and not the least bit concerned about anybody but himself.

They pulled into the compound now. As they neared the gate, she stiffened, then relaxed. "He fixed it," she muttered in amazement.

"Of course," Damon replied. "That's what he does."

"Yeah, well, he'll have to do a lot more of that coming up if he doesn't smarten up," she muttered.

Damon grinned. "Just relax. We got you with us, so we got this."

She glared at him but sighed. When they got out, she stopped in front of the compound, looked around, and pointed. "I need to go over there." She headed off at a fast clip. Damon and Trevor fell in by her side, and so did several of Bullard's men. By the time she got to the corner that bothered her, she stopped and surveyed it. "Anybody else feel the electricity coming off this thing?' she asked.

"I do," Damon confirmed. "Not sure exactly what we're looking at though."

"Neither am I," she admitted, "but something started this." She looked back toward the compound. "Did he get ahold of the city to shut down this line?"

At that, one of the other men spoke up. "He's trying, but they're arguing against it."

She raised one eyebrow. "Arguing?"

"It'll shut down power to a lot of people," he explained, "so they won't do it without proof."

"Proof?" she repeated. "Are you serious?" He just nodded. She looked back at Trevor. "What proof do I need to give them?"

He snorted. "Something that doesn't cause a lot of damage and won't reflect badly on Bullard."

"That doesn't give me much for options."

"I understand," Trevor agreed, "but we're trying to get along, remember?"

"No," she corrected. "*You* are trying to get along. I gave that up when Bullard threatened to not let me out of here." Several of the other men stiffened at that, and she turned and glared at them. "I don't give a shit what you think about that. Believe me that I'm only concerned about self-preservation at the moment."

"So are we," replied one of the men. "We have family, friends, and children here, so, if you can do anything to stop whatever is going on, just do it."

She sighed, then walked over to one of the power lines and stretched out a hand to it.

Trevor called out, "Are you sure you want to do that?"

"No, of course I don't want to do that," she replied in exasperation, "but nobody else can."

He walked over and placed his hand on her shoulder to help ground her.

She frowned. "It shouldn't be that bad."

"*Shouldn't be* is a whole different story than *will be*," he muttered. "Once that energy hits you, it could cause a lot of damage—to you."

She shrugged. "Maybe that's an easy answer to everything too." And she immediately grabbed hold of the power line.

Nothing happened at first, then came a weird rumbling, and sparks started to fly. She held on another minute, and Trevor felt the power surging through her. Yet he had no idea just what she had done.

"You can disconnect now," she told him. "That should be enough for the city officials to act now."

Trevor let his hand drop and took several steps back, grateful that he and Reeni were alive. If that had happened without her around, he knew full well the result wouldn't have been the same.

Two of the other men walked closer, and she held up a hand. "Careful, a lot of power flows through here, still through me and Trevor as well." She turned to face everyone. "We'll come toward you very slowly, but you need to contact the city and tell them to get their ass over here."

"It's already done," Bullard announced, suddenly appearing in front of her. "Did you just set off a power shortage?"

"No, I don't do that. All I do is see energy, so really what I do is completely useless."

He frowned at her. "It doesn't look useless to us. I'm not

sure what all is going on here, but it seems as if it's the opposite of useless."

"But the trouble is, I can't stop this mess. I can tell you that something funky is going on, but I can't even tell you exactly what is happening," she muttered in a disgusted tone of voice. "I don't ever get full information. I just get bits and pieces. Right now those bits and pieces tell me that whoever is playing with electricity is targeting you guys for whatever reason. Bullard anyway," she added, with an eyeroll. At that comment came a snort behind Reeni. She turned to see Leia, looking a bit abashed, and Reeni frowned. "Sorry."

"Not at all," Leia declared, with a smile. "Believe me that Bullard can irritate all of us at times, but he is all heart and only looking to protect us."

Reeni nodded. "I'm glad you believe that." Hearing sirens heading their way, Reeni muttered, "Good thing." She then moved away. "You really don't want me around here when they come in asking what the hell happened."

"Could you even explain anything to them?" Trevor asked.

"Nope, I sure couldn't." And she stepped farther back and away, but closer to Trevor.

He grinned at her and suggested, "Do you want to put on that *little old helpless me* look?"

"Gee, that's no problem," she muttered. "That's what's expected, isn't it?"

Trevor thought she seemed curious and frightened, definitely not the one who had instigated a power shortage or surge or overload or whatever she did.

Leia laughed. "Come on inside. I've got coffee on."

"Coffee would be good. ... Is Dave around?"

"Dave's in the kitchen." Leia seemed puzzled. "Why?"

"If he's in the kitchen, that means there might be food, or maybe there will be soon, right?"

"There's always food here," Leia stated. "After whatever you just did here, I presume you'll need to plow through some."

Reeni shrugged. "Yeah, though it would have been worse if Trevor hadn't grounded me."

"Is that what he does?"

"That's what he did," she declared, with a fading grin. "The ground allows the energy to flow into the ground, so he helps to center it, to direct it, even though he doesn't know that's what he's doing."

"So, I presume what he did was offer you stability?"

"Yes, that's exactly it," she stated, smiling at Leia.

"We've run into other gifted people here," she explained, with a half laugh. "Somebody working here with me as a nurse had quite the abilities too. We had hoped she would stay with us, and she's talking about coming back for a while, which would be great. She had healing abilities such as we've never seen before."

"Yeah, and the minute you've seen it once, somebody else comes along with something else you've never seen," she murmured.

"Yeah, like you." Leia smiled. "We're just so happy to see you."

Reeni didn't know what to do with the emotions that Leia's words stirred up within. That sense of truth so evident to Leia made Reeni uncomfortable.

Leia nodded. "You haven't had a whole lot of good things in your life lately, have you?" she asked, as she led the way.

Trevor kept close to Reeni, while nodding at Leia's perceptive insights.

Leia continued. "And I'm sorry for whatever happened between you and Bullard. It would only have been because he's worried about us."

"Yep," Reeni conceded, "that makes sense." But there was still no give in her tone.

She knew that to give in right now to all these emotions, good and bad, could be catastrophic when she had so much else going on in her world. Her father was the biggest threat to her sanity right now. So it was far better to keep everybody out, keep them as allies yet at a distance, and just let it all be. Right now, she did need food though, particularly after that interaction with the live power line. She asked Trevor, "Did you feel any of that?"

"Yep, I sure did," he declared, looking down at his hand that had been on Reeni's shoulder throughout the whole event. "Never would have thought I could hold that level of electricity in my hand and not get burned."

"Yet we were grounded," Reeni stated, pointing that out.

"We were, and for somebody who doesn't understand very much about how this all works, it seems funny to hear you say that."

She glared at him but silently walked into the kitchen.

Dave looked up with a big smile, then bolted to his feet and gave her a gentle hug. "Here you are to the rescue again, and I, for one, am very grateful."

She sighed. "Still not sure how much I helped."

"Of course not, but apparently you just did. I saw what happened out there," he shared. "Are you okay?"

"I'm fine but ... hungry." Her stomach growled, as if on cue.

His face lit up. "And that is definitely part of my domain. Go sit. and I'll bring you a hot cup of coffee and some food."

While she sat nearby and watched, Dave brought out lasagna from one of the ovens and a huge salad from the fridge. He quickly served her a large portion of each and placed the food in front of her. "Go ahead and get started. The others will be along in a few minutes."

"Bullard's back too," Reeni added.

Dave nodded. "Good." Then he added in a sympathetic tone, "You really don't need to fear him."

She just glared at him, and he returned to the counter, filling serving dishes. Trevor sat down beside her, looking at the meal in front of her and smiled. "You should ask Dave for some too," she suggested. "You used up a lot of energy grounding me."

"Not as much as you did though," he noted cheerfully. "I'm doing okay."

A plate of food was placed in front of him very quickly too. "Thanks, Dave. I don't know what we would do without you," he noted.

"You would all starve," Dave declared instantly, making them burst out laughing. "Yet we all have our special gifts, and are doing what we can in an ugly situation."

"Yeah," Trevor agreed. "That is very true."

"Do we have any more information as to who it is, what's going on, and why?" Dave asked.

Trevor looked to Reeni, and she shook her head. "Nope, other than the threat of a second bomb being around here, I don't know anything about that. At least not yet. I usually feel the energy gathering before any explosions happen. So I'm waiting for that, then I can follow the energy to the bomb. At least I hope so."

"The way you did at the apartment building?" Dave noted.

She nodded. "All I can tell you now is that I sense energy coming from far across town. It's not here yet."

"I'm glad you came back," Dave said, with a smile. "Eat up now. You don't need to wait for the others."

"It's still not resolved though. All I did was ensure the power company had to come out. That won't stop this intruder."

"So, you're thinking it was sabotage? Somebody messed with the power box?"

Reeni nodded. "It was sabotage at the power box, and that leads here to the house. What comes after this, I don't know for sure." She shrugged. "That's what you guys are supposed to do, not me. It's all I can do to handle the shit I have to handle as it is."

Then she picked up her fork and took her first bite. She sighed happily and started plowing into the food.

TREVOR WATCHED REENI eat. He ate a whole lot slower than Reeni did, but she was eating fast enough that he was a little worried that she could keep it down.

When she finally slowed, several others appeared shocked at how she ate so much, so fast. She frowned at them and returned to her food, although eating much slower now. Then she stopped and sighed. "I'm showing really bad table manners, aren't I?" She looked over at Trevor. "Are you enjoying it?"

"Absolutely," he replied, with a huge smile. "It's excellent, but then the food here is always good."

"Ha," Dave noted, "I can't even remember the last time I fed you."

"It's been a while," Trevor said cheerfully, "but I sure haven't forgotten."

At that came noise from the entrance, and several more people arrived. Bullard stepped in, and Reeni stiffened and glared at him. He glared right back.

Trevor placed his hand over hers. "He's not here to work against you. Nobody here is the enemy. Just remember that."

"He's not here for me," she declared. "Therefore, he's against me."

Bullard looked at her in astonishment. "No, I'm not," he argued in exasperation. "I've never been against you. You came here, as an unknown factor, which I told you before, and the fact that you blew apart my gate while I stood there watching was extremely disconcerting," he explained. "However, I would much rather have you on my side than against me. So I do apologize for my bad behavior at the gate before."

She stared at Bullard, her gaze narrowed.

Trevor squeezed her hand. "And, yes, that's Bullard's honest opinion, and it comes from his heart." She shot Trevor a questioning look, and he nodded at her. "It's not easy for Bullard to admit he's wrong, you know? He really loved that gate."

She snorted. "It needed fixing anyway."

Bullard frowned at her and asked, "How did you know it needed fixing?"

"There was a glitch in the electronic circuit, so I did you a favor."

He stared at her. "How did you know there was a glitch in the circuit?"

"Because I could see the energy. It was crossed." She frowned at him. "And, no. … I don't know how, so don't bother asking. All I can tell you is that something was crossed."

He frowned. "I put that gate in myself."

"Yeah, well, maybe somebody else tampered with it," she stated. "Did you ever consider that?"

"Before then, no, but now? … Definitely," he replied, studying her. "You got any other tidbits of information?"

She shook her head. "No, my brain is numb from that last bit of electrical work I just did. So my brain needs to reset, and I need more food, so you'll have to excuse me."

He looked down at her empty plate, shook his head, and asked, "Do you burn through food at that rate all the time?"

"Only if I have to touch electricity," she murmured. "Or shift it—for want of a better word." She could see the question on everybody's faces. She looked over at Damon and saw him grinning at her. She groaned. "I don't have answers and don't know how all this shit works," she admitted. "I can only tell you what I do know when something hits my radar. If you want further explanations about electrical and all that, I'm sure you can find it online."

"These guys happen to be specialists in all that," Damon told her, now laughing openly. "The thing is, they can't see the electricity in the same way as you do."

She shook her head. "Why would you go into a field where you can't see it?" she asked curiously.

Trevor chuckled. "Yet 99.999 percent of the world can't see it either, remember? They're going on blind faith that it won't kill them."

"But it will kill them if they do the wrong thing."

"Exactly, which is why we try hard not to do the *wrong*

thing," Bullard noted, staring at her. "But you can see it?"

"Sure. I can see the lines all through this house. … Some people would say it isn't terribly healthy for a pregnant woman," Reeni pointed out, turning to face Leia.

Leia stared at her. "I'm not pregnant."

Reeni's eyebrows shot up at that. Then she shrugged and went back to eating.

Damon looked over at Leia, while Leia stared at Bullard, and Damon laughed. "Or maybe you are."

Leia shook her head. "That's not in the plan right now." She turned to Reeni. "Seriously?"

"I'm just telling you about the energy," she said, with a shrug. "I see energy from you to your belly, and it zips over to Bullard. So that child, that pregnancy, is his. Beyond that I know nothing."

Everybody else started to grin.

Reeni added, "I'm not sure why you would be upset by it, though. Obviously you guys are into family life, so why would you be less than pleased?"

"Oh, I'm absolutely thrilled." Leia beamed, her hand covering her flat belly, "but I know, for Bullard, it'll be fairly stressful."

"Yeah, the last pregnancy didn't go so well," he muttered, glaring at his wife.

"It went fine," she declared, still beaming at him. "Remember that we wanted more than one pregnancy anyway."

He shook his head. "No, *you* did. I just want you alive and well."

At that, the conversation fell quiet for a moment, as everybody contemplated that reality.

Damon asked Reeni, "What about other electrical systems?"

"If it's an electrical system, I can see it," she explained. "It's not that I see energy as much as I see the electrical energy around it. I tried to explain that to you before, but I know it didn't come across so well. Every time I try to explain it, it gets convoluted."

"No, I just find it interesting that you see electrical energy, but you don't see any other energy," he shared, "because, in theory, there's energy swarming through this room because we're all energized beings. So, to have just electrical energy show up differently on your radar is ..."

"Odd," she stated in a challenging voice.

"*Unique*," he clarified, with a grin. "Stop trying to take offense so quickly."

She stared at him and groaned. "Yeah, it's an ingrained habit."

"Yet you came here all on your own will to warn us," Leia pointed out, also grinning broadly.

TREVOR UNDERSTOOD WHAT Damon was trying to say, and it was interesting that Reeni didn't get it. "I wonder if it's a blockage on your part," he suggested, "as if you expect to see one thing, so that's all you see."

"Maybe," she acknowledged. "This room is floating in energy, and we're all energy, but it's not as if I see all the lines going from one person to another."

"Yet you just saw it going from Leia to Bullard."

She nodded. "But I think that's just because ..." She lifted a hand and waved it around, and an immediate crackle bounced around the room. Several people gasped, and she shrugged. "I'm still charged, so I'm seeing a little more than I would normally."

"Right," Damon noted. "So, can we utilize that leftover charge? What do you see that is a little more enhanced right now?"

She stared at Damon, puzzled. "I'm sorry? What do you mean?"

"If you were to put down the food for a moment," he said, with a note of humor, "and we were to walk through this place, would you see other areas of trouble? Like that supposed second bomb?"

"You mean, because it's not just potentially electrical right now?" Without waiting for his answer, she hopped up and nodded. With at least twelve of them following behind her, Trevor very close to her side, they walked through the offices and up and around the multiple apartments. Only when they came back to the server room did she stop and stare. "I thought you guys fixed that."

"Fixed what?" Bullard asked.

She pointed at the server. "The server."

He stared at her. "We did."

She shook her head. "No, you didn't, or, if you did, whoever did this before, did it again. Have you guys had anybody here in this house? Anybody since I was here before, who could have had any access to this?"

Bullard shook his head. "No, when we're in lockdown, nobody comes in or out."

"I did," she declared.

He glared at her. "Yeah, but you made your own entrance," he noted in a dry tone.

She nodded. "I did because I needed to, but I wonder if somebody took advantage of that." At that, Bullard stiffened beside her. She nodded. "It feels very much as if whatever happened to that server before is happening again. Somebody's hijacking it, but this time electronically." She looked over at his team. "You guys have somebody in your system right now, so you may want to fix that."

Several men jumped on computers, and keyboards were pounded on almost as quickly. She turned to Trevor. "It feels different from last time."

"In what way?" he asked curiously.

She thought about it. "It feels as if it was online last time, like somebody set up something, thought that it would work, but we thwarted it, so somebody is now trying it another way. Potentially … why does Bullard still have internet? Didn't all of that go down?"

"Yes, but it just came back up again about twenty minutes ago."

She pondered that. "Does it normally come up that fast?"

Everybody shared a frown.

Bullard replied, "No. We do have a backup generator, but that's electrical."

She pondered that. "Maybe you should show me where that is."

Bullard led the way through to another part of the compound. As she walked into the rear of the room, she stopped and pointed at a power box up against the wall. "What is that?"

Bullard replied, "It's part of the backup system."

She nodded. "Did it get serviced recently?"

His face darkened. "Yes, it absolutely did." He called someone on his phone and started assessing something on the panel.

She looked back at Damon. "Can I leave now and go

back to the food?"

"I think so," he said, with a smile. "I presume you found something wrong with that."

"I don't know that something is necessarily wrong with it," she clarified. "If that's right, then … it's not anything I would have recognized as right." She raised both hands. "I get it. That's no help."

"It's a huge help," Bullard corrected, "because it was just serviced, and it was not the regular person."

She nodded. "He would have had access to the house for a little bit, and everybody probably treated him as trustworthy, since he supposedly had clearance from a company you guys use all the time." She shrugged. "You know how all that works. However, the person who came and did this? Yeah, something is there. I just don't know what." Then she turned to Trevor. "If you know how this mausoleum of a place works, do you want to help me back to the kitchen, please?"

He nodded and reached out a hand. She put hers in it and squeezed his. "You need more food?" he asked her.

"No, I'm fine. It just feels off. Everything down here feels off."

She shivered and then looked at Damon. "Does it feel off to you?"

"It does," he agreed, looking at the backup generator. "And that's a big unit."

"It is, but it's *off*, as in *wrong*." Then she laughed. "I see what you guys mean. Maybe I could use a little bit more vocabulary."

"No, *off* works in this instance," Damon confirmed, as he looked over at Bullard, "because she's right. That's what I feel too."

Bullard stared at Damon. "Just *off?*"

"Yeah, just *off*," he repeated, "as in somebody's tinkered with it. If that thing is meant to kick in, I suspect when it does or did, something else is meant to kick in too."

"It did kick in though," Bullard stated. "When the power went out just recently, it did kick in."

"*Right*," Damon replied, but he didn't like the sound of that. He looked over at Reeni.

She nodded. "So, whatever is happening just started to happen now. So, we've got the big *boom* still to come."

Nobody liked what she said. Trevor looked around the small room and asked Bullard, "What does this connect to? Names and places quickly."

"Everything," Bullard declared, with a sigh. "Absolutely everything."

"Then you need to check everything that's connected to it," Trevor stated.

With that, teams of men spread out, and Trevor slowly led her back up to the kitchen. As she got into the kitchen, she sat down, her hands suddenly chilled. She frowned at him. "Something feels wrong."

"You're right, but they're on it now," he said in a reassuring tone of voice. She nodded but didn't look at all convinced, and he could see why. A lot of things were going on. He looked over at Dave. "You need to keep a full watch on the compound."

Dave nodded, and his face was grim. "Yeah, message received on that count. We have a lot of women in residence, and several of them are pregnant."

"Of course, and somebody's trying to hurt more than just one," she shared, frowning, then she shook her head. "I don't normally get insights, so I'm not sure what this is either."

"Don't worry about it," Trevor said, "just let any information flow."

"What about you?"

"I was hoping I could do a scan, scope outside the area, and search for any irregularities."

"Oh, yeah, that's a good idea," she agreed. "That's one of the things you can do too, isn't it?"

He smiled. "Sometimes, though not always, I need a few minutes to get my thoughts in order." He looked over at Dave. "You okay to take over here if I just zone out?"

Fascinated, Dave nodded slowly. "Yeah, you do what you need to do. The rest of us don't get it, but neither do we have those abilities. So fly at it and keep us safe."

And, with that, Trevor shifted free of his body and floated up. He went higher, out of the building. He searched the compound, looking to see what was bothering him. Yet it wasn't just him; it was Reeni and Damon too. Something was *off*. Trevor wasn't sure what and wasn't sure how, but definitely something was going on here that he didn't recognize.

When he heard Terk in the back of his mind, calling for him, Trevor replied, *I'm here*, and opened up a mental door to Terk.

There's definite sabotage at Bullard's compound, Terk shared urgently. *We've sorted and assessed some of it and came down to a certain location. I'm doing an overseeing arc right now, taking a closer look at what I can find. Stay a little closer to Bullard's home and ensure that nothing is happening on a one-to-one basis,* Terk suggested, *because definitely something is wrong. I don't know what it is, but I can feel it from here. I just phoned and warned Bullard.*

Trevor agreed. *Yeah, everybody here is on full alert. Something's happening, something's coming, but we don't know what. Reeni has been getting warnings too, but we don't know where the trouble is coming from, which makes all of us feel pretty damn useless.*

We never get full answers, Terk noted, his tone calm and reassuring. *All any of us can do is pull up the information as it presents itself and ensure that we're all ready to react fast enough to deal with whatever is going on. Yet, just as soon as you find out one thing, you have to plan for it to be something completely different. It's never quite so simple in Bullard's world.*

Or ours, Trevor noted.

Yeah, so does that mean you'll come work for me?

Maybe. I answered the call when you put it out, though I still can't quite believe you used a beacon.

Yeah, I've rescinded it now. He chuckled. *But I did get a few other people contacting me. So maybe it's all good.*

Maybe, he murmured. *If you got any seers over there, we could use them right now. Something's not only wrong here in wonderland, it's straight-up ugly.*

And, with that, he disconnected from Terk and sent his energy far and wide, looking for a source of the trouble. He found himself very quickly atop that same apartment building that had been evacuated. He realized that they would have to head back there, even if it had been evacuated once and cleared that time. Something was still here that needed to be assessed, that needed to be found, and quickly at that.

He zipped back into his body, bolted to his feet, and looked at Dave. "I need a team, and I need it now."

Bullard walked into the kitchen and came straight to his side. "Where are we going?"

"To that same apartment building where they just found the bombmaking supplies," he said.

"You mean, the one that the police have us locked out of because of the bombs? Why would you want to go back there?"

Damon raced in. "What's going on?"

"We have to get to that apartment building again," Trevor shared. "I'm not sure if we still have the same person doing this there, but definitely some information about him is in that apartment, so we need to get in there."

He strode quickly out to the parking lot, and Reeni followed him. He looked at her and shook his head. "You need to stay here." Her jaw jutted out at him. "I get it. You don't want to be left behind, and I appreciate that, but I need you to keep an eye on everybody here. You'll be the one in the line of fire if there's an imminent attack. We'll get over there as fast as we can and hurry back. I'm leaving, taking a team with me. You've got Bullard and the rest of his men here."

"You also know that you'll be up against something there too," she declared. He frowned at her, and she shrugged. "Yeah, I don't know anything," she muttered. "Just things. Always just things."

"That's fine. Keep the communication open, and I'll check back in a few minutes."

She stared at him with a woebegone expression, and he smiled, leaned over, and gave her a goodbye kiss. Then just like that, Trevor and his team were gone.

CHAPTER 8

REENI TURNED AROUND and stared at the compound, finding Bullard with a note of contrition in his expression.

He nodded. "I know you wanted to go with Trevor, not so much to be with him but to not be here."

She shrugged, then nodded. "Yeah, I do have this thing against being held prisoner." She glared at him. "Never again, … not in this lifetime."

"I would never have done that," he said. "However, something about your attitude collided with my frustration, not knowing how to protect my family. I know I behaved badly, and I was totally out of line."

"Yeah," she agreed, "that's the only reason I'm here now."

He smiled and nodded at her. "So … peace?" Then he held out his hand.

She winced at that, as she stared and then groaned.

"We start over," Bullard stated.

She slowly nodded and held out her hand. And, with that handshake, a little sense of peace came into her soul. She looked back at his compound and asked, "Did you ever figure out what was going on with that generator?"

"Definitely some electrical components are inside that shouldn't be there, yet it's no second bomb," he told her.

"They're tearing it apart now, seeing if they can hack it backward."

"Oh, they can hack it backward, but they've got these Bluetooth things all throughout the house."

He stared at her. "Bluetooth things?"

"Yeah, you know, when they put light switches on different walls, and you don't have to move the wiring because they can just use a Bluetooth connector now?" she explained. "They've got those attached for triggering this thing. I presume you found the powdery chemicals on some of the electrical components?"

He nodded. "We did, yes. and I presume they were the same chemicals from the apartment with the bomb-making materials, but we don't know that yet."

"We do know that," she clarified, with a shrug. "At least I presume that's why they all took off."

"My understanding is that they think somebody is still there at the apartment."

She hesitated. "Yeah, that would be my guess too. Somebody or something."

"You really don't have any control over your ... *ability*, do you?" Bullard asked.

"It's not about control," she stated, looking at him. "I don't necessarily even understand what I can and cannot do. I'm just a messenger, and that ends up being a problem."

"I've heard that a time or two from Terk," Bullard murmured, as he stared off into the distance.

"You can go back inside and do whatever you need to do," she said, with a wave of her hand. "You don't have to babysit me."

"I'm not babysitting," he clarified, looking at her. "The team is handling it."

"What about Leia?"

"Leia's lying down. She's still in shock."

"She really didn't know, did she?"

"No, she didn't know." And then he grinned boyishly. "I told her, *No more kids* because she had such a terrible time with the last one, but she was bound and determined to have more."

"Three more," Reeni announced. He looked at her and visibly paled. She shrugged, knowing she had no filter and yet knowing she was right. "Sorry, I could be wrong," she added.

His gaze narrowed. "You and Terk, … you are both irritating as hell."

"Yeah, it's the precog side."

"I thought you didn't do precog."

"I don't." And then she groaned. "Jesus, I don't do anything consistently. I … seem to be a wild card in that regard, which is one of the reasons I don't think Terk would want me on his team."

"Terk will figure out all that. Now, from what I've heard, we've got a problem with your father. Tell me more about that."

"You don't have a problem. I do."

"Tell me what's going on."

"Nothing new really. When I was a minor, he had control over all the medical decisions and finances. As I got older, he realized he was losing that control. When these *things* manifested, these abilities, I didn't know to keep my mouth shut, thinking, for once, he would be thrilled with me. Instead he was horrified and used it to have me locked up in a mental institution. He's done nothing but try to control me ever since. When he does capture me, I get imprisoned, until I can find a way out again," she explained. "I've been free for the last four years now, but, because the police called him, now he's in town, looking to grab me all over again."

"What does he gain by holding you? Are you financially independent?"

"I am, in a way," she replied cautiously. "My grandmother set up money for me, but it's not in the name that he knows me by, so he hasn't been able to find it. Yet he has a ton of money himself," she added quickly, "so I don't know if he cares so much about money as he does about power and control over me."

Bullard nodded. "Have you seen these documents he supposedly has?"

"No, I haven't. Nobody will let me see anything," she stated bitterly. "And they're all signed, sealed, and delivered by lawyers. I'm sure Dad paid plenty for them, and yet, when I was a minor, he probably didn't have to do much of anything, but, as I grew up, … everything changed."

"And this is yet another instance where he's trying to maintain that control, which is interesting."

"I think it's also partly because he doesn't want his good name sullied with the craziness I bring."

"Hey, all families have at least one crazy among them," Bullard declared. "It's part and parcel of it."

She snorted at that. "*Great*, that makes me feel *so* much better," she muttered, glaring at him.

"I didn't mean that you were crazy," he corrected. "However, if you look at any of the wealthy old-money families, there's always a skeleton somewhere. The fact that your father is trying to hide it just means that something even more is going on."

"Like?"

"Does he have some of these abilities himself?"

She stared at him. "I don't think so. Why would he act like that if he did?"

"Maybe the abilities terrify him, or maybe he found something that he didn't like in his future."

"I don't know. He would never have talked to me about it anyway, so it's not as if I'll get answers."

"No? I've got people making inquiries into it right now," he shared, "and we'll see what they come back with. They are quite discreet too."

"Inquiries into this nonsense with my father?" she asked in astonishment. "Why would you spend your resources on me?"

He nodded. "You help me, and I help you," he stated. "That's the way the world works."

"Usually it's not," she argued, staring at him. "Usually it's you help somebody, and they just get up and run."

He laughed. "That's why Damon and Trevor are here. We needed help, so we put out the word, and they came running. In my world, that's what families do, and that's what friends are for."

"I don't know about that," she said. "That's not the kind of friends and family I've ever known."

"Except for Trevor and your grandmother."

At that, her heart softened, and she nodded. "Trevor is a friend. And my grandmother is definitely an exception. Some people are just solid gold, and that was her."

And, with that, Bullard led her back into the kitchen, where Dave was.

He looked at her and asked, "Hungry?"

She shook her head. "I'm okay now, though I wouldn't

mind some more coffee." She sat down near the sideboard, and, just as she was about to take a sip, he stepped out with a trayful of cinnamon buns. She shook her head. "Jesus, you must do nothing but cook."

"My partner and I both do," he admitted, with a chuckle. "She runs a catering business that we work together on."

Reeni smiled at him. "I'm glad to hear that. How are you finding life these days?" she asked impulsively.

He looked at her. "It's great, as always."

She nodded slowly. "It's a change for you, right?"

Bullard sat down beside her, looking at her curiously, and then back over at Dave. "If you mean Dave's been through a lot in his life, the answer is yes."

"I can see that, just one of those precog flashes. Two little boys?"

Dave looked at her, then shook his head. "I lost one of each."

She stared at him and flushed. "Oh." She looked over at Bullard.

He stared at her for a moment and then started to grin. "Seriously?" he asked.

She shrugged.

Bullard looked back at Dave. "So, is she pregnant?"

"Who?" Dave asked, walking over with his coffee in his hand, and sat down beside them. "I'm not sure what you're even talking about."

Bullard chuckled. "You heard about Reeni's announcement earlier today, didn't you?"

"What announcement?" he asked. "I've been in the kitchen all morning."

Reeni shrugged. "It was just something that popped up when I saw Leia."

Dave looked around and asked, "Is she okay?" He turned to Bullard, with a frown. "I know she's been really tired lately."

"With good reason, as apparently she's pregnant, according to this one at least." Bullard nodded at Reeni.

Dave looked at her in delight. "Is Leia pregnant?"

"She is, but I guess she didn't know, so I feel bad for being the one to announce it."

Dave burst out laughing. "It's probably better this way, since Bullard here wouldn't have been terribly impressed either way."

"Yeah, but, since it's a fact already," Bullard said, with a shrug, "you know we'll deal."

"Of course you will, and you also know that she wanted several children," Dave reminded Bullard.

"According to our guest here, who apparently gets these intuitive precogs, we have three more in our future."

Dave smiled at her. "That is wonderful news," he declared, with a big grin.

"That's why I'm mentioning your boys," she added.

Dave shook his head. "Sorry, what do you mean?"

"She means you," Bullard pointed out, his grin wider and deeper than before. "I think she's saying you're about to become a daddy."

He stared at Bullard, then back at her. "What?"

It never ceased to amaze her how it could be a complete surprise, but she shrugged and nodded. "Yeah, twin boys."

He didn't know what to say, just bolted from the room.

She groaned. "This is why I should keep my mouth shut."

"Oh, I don't know," Bullard countered. "Since you let the cat out of the bag in my personal life, I think it's only fair that other people get the same surprises."

She glared at him. "That's just because you're happy to share the pain."

"The pain was the delivery and the nightmare at the same time," he replied. "The compound was under attack then too."

She stared at him, her mouth gaping open. "And here I thought your security would be better than that." He shot her a hard look at that. She shrugged. "Okay, so you don't like hearing that, but—"

"Yes, I know, but you're still right. We've obviously had another lapse in here, and that is something I'll get to the bottom of very quickly."

"You let in a repairman who isn't your regular," she noted. "That's all it takes, somebody who supposedly was nice and easy on the eyes because it's something you had to get done anyway."

"The generator's too big to lift," he explained, "and I've been traveling a lot, so I okayed it. I don't even remember who I okayed to go ahead and get it done."

"Does it matter? They weren't responsible."

"Are you sure?" he asked. "It worries me that our family here has expanded so much. I just don't want to find out I brought in someone only to have them be part of the betrayal."

"Nobody here was part of it," she stated. "I've checked everyone here."

He nodded. "How can you be so sure?"

"Energy."

"But you work with electrical systems."

"Yeah, I know," she muttered, with a sigh. "Yet, for some reason, what I'm getting here is a whole lot more. I don't have the slightest idea why."

"Maybe because you're opening yourself up to more," Bullard suggested. "Just something I've learned from Terk."

"Maybe," she muttered, "but that'll just confuse the issue. If I don't know what I'm getting, it will just be harder for me to decipher what I'm seeing."

"Or maybe you'll just end up getting a whole lot more information, and you'll be fine. But I have one more question. What about other team members who haven't been here at the compound? Have you read their energy?" While they sat there, Bullard's phone rang. "Eton," he barked into the phone. "What did you find out? ... Wait. She's right here. I'll put you on Speakerphone."

"Your father definitely does have paperwork in place," Eton began. "The doctor who helped him set it up has his own clinic."

Bullard nodded. "Yeah, I'm not surprised."

"Whether he helped him legitimately, thinking she would be a problem, I don't know," Eton added, "but it's definitely in place."

Bullard looked at her, then at his phone. "Eton, what's the atmosphere around her father?"

"Nobody likes him, for one. He's definitely a hard-ass. More about the bottom line and not particularly fussy about methodology. He's big in the business community and worth several hundred million, so I doubt her money would make any difference to him. So it's probably more about control and image. There's something odd about the mother. She was in a sanatorium as well, whether that's because she needs it or because it was more convenient to get her out of the way, I don't know," he shared.

She stared at Bullard in horror. "My mother?'

Bullard nodded. "That's what it sounds like."

"That's right," Eton confirmed. "The mother is definitely there, and I heard some talk that the sister may not be very stable either."

"Yet she's very stable," Reeni proclaimed bitterly. "At least as stable as anybody can be, considering they're dealing with him."

Eton's tone was apologetic as he replied, "Sorry, I've obviously got more digging to do on much of this."

"Is there any way to break what he's got in place?" Bullard asked.

"Sure, there always is. Reeni, the mother, the sister, they would all have to be tested of course, but, as long as each are of sound mind, then there's absolutely no reason the paperwork couldn't be rescinded. It's done all the time. Sometimes people are appointed a guardian to look after all this, and sometimes that works out, and sometimes it doesn't," he pointed out, with a wry tone. "Think of all the popular singers and pop stars and how that doesn't work out sometimes."

She snorted. "The only interaction my father wants with me is to control me. I don't think my money matters, since its nothing to him, although everybody else in my family gets an inheritance too," she explained. "His mother bypassed him and gave her money to me and my sister. Then my mother's family has a trust set up to go through my mother, so I don't know how that'll work out for Dad."

"It could be why he's making sure that he locks everybody up tight, so he can keep you all under his control just to get at the total inheritance," Bullard pointed out.

She frowned at that. "I suppose."

"Have you ever seen any of the wills?"

"No, only what I've been told. Dad's mother left nothing to Dad, so her estate goes to me and my sister directly. Then my mother's family left everything to us—to my mother and my sister and me," she shared, "So we have zero contact with any of it because my father controls it all."

"Any way to find out if there's been a change at all along those lines?" Bullard asked. "Because it's quite possible that when you and your sister turn a certain age, you are supposed to get something."

"When I turn thirty," Reeni stated.

"When you turn thirty, what happens?"

She shrugged. "My grandmother told me it was all coming to me."

He whistled. "When you say, *all?*"

"I don't know what that means. I don't know if that's just my grandmother's money or my mother's trust money," she shared. "Again … I haven't ever seen anything."

"But that's a really good angle to go on," Eton noted. "I'll be back in touch as soon as I find out anything." And, with that, he ended the call.

Bullard looked at her. "How are you doing for money?"

"I'm fine. I have a special fund that my grandmother set up, … *his* mother."

"Maybe your grandmother set up something else too."

"Not if he knew about it. It must be something she did on the sly. She was all for protecting me, for providing for me, but my father had her under lock and key by the end of her days."

"But she did bypass him once, as you mentioned, so she could have managed it a second time. And you mentioned it's *his* mother?"

She nodded. "Yes, but she was very good friends with

my mother's parents as well. They were best friends for a long time."

"Then what happened?"

"My mother's family, several of them, were killed in a car accident," she explained. "Then a couple people in the family had cancer, and all sorts of diseases started popping up, things like that. I don't even know how many are left at this point."

"But maybe your dad does, and what if the family money all comes to you, and you're the one he can't control?"

"All the more reason to stay free of him," she muttered, "because, as soon as he finds me, I'll end up in the same place as my mother, maybe not even the same place. At least there I could see her."

"Would you want to?"

Reeni frowned at that. "I don't have any way to know how much she's had to do with any of this. Maybe she had nothing to do with it at all, and it's all been my father's doing," she suggested. "So I don't know what the answer to that question is. I would really like a chance to ensure she's okay—and my sister as well."

When she explained more about her sister's marriage, Bullard stared at her in shock. "That's very feudal."

"It's very much my father," she stated. "He will fight tooth and nail to maintain control. It would make more sense if some massive inheritance was coming to somebody. I just don't know who."

"How old is your sister?"

"She would have turned thirty last year," she replied.

"In that case, he probably has that one locked down, at least for the moment. Maybe now he wants to ensure that yours is locked down too."

She winced, then nodded. "Yeah, that sounds very much like him." And then she stared at Bullard in anticipation. "So, is there anything we can do to stop it?"

Bullard gave her a beaming nod. "Of course something can always be done. He won't like it much."

She stared at him, a sliver of hope unfurling in her chest for the first time in a very long while, and she whispered, "That sounds even better."

TREVOR WAS ACCOMPANIED by Damon and two men of Bullard's, Jerome and Kano.

Those two looked at Terk's men and asked, "So now what?"

Trevor winced. "Wouldn't it be nice if we knew," he muttered. He looked over at Damon. "She didn't give any specific directions, did she?"

Damon shook his head. "I didn't hear any."

Trevor asked him, almost grinning, "You want to contact her?"

"Nope, I sure don't. That'll likely set her off."

"What's the point in working with people if they're so touchy?" Jerome asked. "I get she's supposed to have some skills, but I'm not sure the skills are that valuable if you can't count on them."

Surprised, Trevor turned to him. "That would be because you don't understand where she's coming from and what she's been through, so please don't judge her. Yet the reason that we have any intel at all and were brought to this apartment in the first place is because of her. We never had a chance to inspect this apartment, so, from my perspective, that is something that we should have done regardless."

Damon nodded. "That's a good point. We can sit here and judge as much as we want, but it doesn't change the fact that she did bring us here in the first place. It's obviously a place that we needed to look into. If anything remains here, as she says it does, then we must find it and find it fast." With that settled, Damon led the way up to the apartment.

"What are we doing about the cops if they show up?" Jerome asked at his side.

He looked over at him and smiled. "I'm not sure how long you've worked for Bullard, but I highly doubt the cops being here are much of an issue."

Jerome shrugged. "I haven't worked for him that long," he replied easily. "However, as a citizen of the world, it's not as if we can just walk around and do what we want to do."

"No, we sure can't," Trevor agreed, studying Jerome with a nod. "But, when local law enforcement doesn't know how to handle people like us, Damon and I and the rest of our team get called in."

"What exactly do you do?" Kano asked curiously.

Trevor shrugged. "It's hard to explain. Let's just call it woo-woo stuff." And, with that, he moved forward, determined to shut off the conversation. He hadn't gotten any *off* feelings from anybody on Bullard's team up until now, and he had to admit that even being questioned like this was uncomfortable. As a matter of fact, that wasn't even much in the way of questioning. It was just somebody who was being asked to go into a building that had been full of bomb-making equipment.

Of course he would have some questions, and he would ask them, as well as question the mind-set of those who prodded them into going back here. That Trevor trusted

Reeni said a lot about where he was at. That Damon trusted her said a lot about her energy. Trevor looked over at Damon to find him frowning at the elevator.

Damon shook his head. "I'm not sure about you but no elevators for me."

Trevor laughed. "I was just thinking the same thing."

The others looked at him, and Jerome asked, "Why?"

"Because that's the last place you want to be if something goes wrong."

At that, Jerome's face thinned, and he nodded. "Stairs it is then."

As soon as they started walking up, Jerome lagged behind. Damon looked over at him, scrutinizing his face. "You okay?"

"I am," he said, with a shrug. "Funny how even that little bit of questioning makes Reeni's back go up, doesn't it?"

"Oh, it certainly gets mine going," Damon agreed, with a laugh. "Still, I understand Reeni's frustration. Yet, if you don't create a reasonable explanation, you'll always struggle to be believed. So she dives right in, not necessarily in the most efficient manner. She let Bullard know that there was a problem. Now, whether or not he appreciated her delivery," Damon stated, with a smile, "her intel was quite accurate."

"I don't think he appreciated the manner or the fact that she couldn't explain it. Plus, it didn't help that she wasn't part of our team," Jerome added.

At that, Trevor nodded. "Oh, I get that. Terk's team does have that woo-woo factor," he agreed, with half a laugh.

Damon nodded. "When we were working for the government, we were free and clear of all kinds of questions as we were black ops. We could do things without having to justify ourselves. So, if there were problems, we could make a phone call and get assistance in getting out of it. Nowadays we don't have that same umbrella, yet we still expect it. After all, we have certain needs for it, depending on the circumstances."

"This is one of those circumstances," Trevor pointed out, "mostly because we are dealing with local law enforcement on this one. So there's just no way to justify going in here without it. Do you think Bullard cleared this?"

"I hope so," Damon muttered, with a laugh. "Otherwise we could find ourselves answering a few more questions than we might want to."

Trevor winced at that and nodded. "I guess that would be fair, wouldn't it?"

"Oh, I don't know about fair," Damon clarified. "I don't like answering law enforcement questions at the best of times, but I am getting better at it, and I do it more often now than I ever have. As we build relationships around the world, some of that's getting easier too."

"Yet at the scope that you're dealing with, it must be massive," Trevor noted.

Damon nodded. "Yep, and as long as we know that we have some backup, such as MI6 for example, that helps. However, we've done several jobs where they couldn't be involved. So we just had to get the job done and then get the hell out without anybody knowing because, if someone does find out, you're on your own."

Jerome had been quiet for most of this conversation, until now. "The thing is, being on your own with a team like my team behind us is a whole different story than really being on your own because we have all kinds of skills. What's interesting is we don't have anybody quite so … very erratic, and I don't know if that's her actual energy or if it's just the way she perceives things. To think that she has an affinity for electricity is one thing, but I would think that would be something she could carry over to energy as a whole."

"I'm pretty sure Reeni can. She just doesn't know it yet," Trevor interjected, giving him a smile. "So being around Terk and his team, plus your team, she could learn so much more. However, until she can deal with that asshole father of hers, I'm not sure she has the capacity to handle much more. She's already keeping up a ton of energy around her, just to keep him away from her, purely for protection. She just doesn't know it."

"Ah, now that," Damon noted, "would explain the energy I find around her on a regular basis. It's very much of a stay-away thing, but it's very personalized."

"Yeah, personalized for her father, I would think," Trevor agreed. "And, from what we know of him so far, that is with good reason."

"Yeah, you're not kidding. We need to take care of this daddy business before we're done here too."

"It would be good if we could," Trevor stated. "I would go it alone, but I'm not sure that I have the right tools to do so."

"No, don't go it alone," Damon said. "I'm pretty sure that Terk, Bullard, Levi, or somebody has the clout to handle this one in a much better way than we could. It's not so much an energy problem. It's all about power and might and the long reach of justice, so that's a whole different story. The fact that her father goes around having people institutionalized is creepy to begin with, yet I don't find anything unstable mentally about her at all."

"No, neither do I," Trevor stated.

Jerome stared at them. "Are you serious? She appears to be completely unstable from where I sit. Honestly, if it wasn't for you guys, I probably wouldn't be listening to her at all."

Damon shrugged. "In Terk's world, an awful lot is going on out there that we don't know about. Reeni is just one more part of it."

"Maybe," Jerome muttered. "It still doesn't feel right though. Why would you listen to any intel from somebody who's obviously not all there?"

Trevor felt his own back going up at the criticism and at the disdain Jerome had for Reeni. It was fair enough that he should have an opinion. Everybody was entitled to that, but having it leveled at her in such a way didn't feel right. "I didn't realize you felt so strongly about it," Trevor said, gazing at Jerome, still a few steps behind them all.

Damon shot Trevor a hard look, silently reminding him where they were and what they needed to be doing. That was fine, but Trevor didn't have to remain silent and let this young man forget the fact that he was still alive mostly because of Reeni. Jerome obviously didn't see it that way, which was yet another fault line in this whole perception thing with Jerome. "She's saved your life once already."

Jerome looked at him and snorted. "I get it. You're sleeping with her, which honestly seems kind of daring of you in the first place, but definitely not my thing."

"That's fine if it's not your thing," Trevor replied calmly. "And, for the record, we're not sleeping together. We're friends."

"Maybe not yet, but you want to." Jerome huffed. "Same diff."

Trevor stared at him in astonishment. "Wow, that's an

interesting mentality you've got there."

Kano didn't say anything, but he frowned at Jerome.

"It's hardly the same thing," Trevor muttered.

"Sure it is," Jerome argued. "If you want to sleep with her, that's your problem, but you don't have to involve the rest of us in your risky endeavors."

At that, Damon halted and turned to face Jerome. "We don't criticize someone unless they are here to defend themselves. That way faulty thinking like yours can be corrected, and we can all move on as a team, whether one single team or a merged team. Obviously you're not the right person to come here for this job, and it's just as obvious that you are stressed out about going up to the apartment. Why don't you go back outside? You can be on watch duty."

Jerome shook his head. "Hell to that. … No way. I'm coming," he declared. "I'm allowed to have an opinion on this whole nightmare. That is not something you get to stop. Besides, I don't have to listen to you anyway. You're not my boss."

At that retort, Kano chipped in, standing beside Jerome and towering over him. "Maybe not, Jerome, but you do have to listen to me, and I agree with Damon. Your attitude right now isn't conducive to the job, considering we're about to walk into an apartment that could be loaded with bombs. So you're back outside on watch duty, just like Damon said."

Jerome glared at Kano. "That's not fair."

"What's not fair about it?"

"That you're defending that psychic chick," he replied, "when it doesn't have anything to do with you."

Kano stared at him in astonishment. "What are you talking about? They're all part and parcel of the same team, the same skill set. We've utilized their services and worked together many, many times. This is nothing new, so why are you so hyped up now?"

"Yeah, *them*, not her," Jerome repeated in disgust. "Anybody can see that something is seriously wrong with her."

At that Damon added in a threatening tone, "Look, buddy. Either you're leaving now or I'm calling Bullard to come get you. … Your choice."

Flushing in anger, Jerome turned and headed back down the stairs. As he left and went down several flights, Trevor waited until he was out of sight, then he turned and asked Kano, "How long has he worked for you?"

"Not long enough, apparently," Kano grumbled, his tone tight. "Sorry about that. His behavior is not the kind that any of us would condone."

Trevor added, "Which is also why it's interesting that he's spouting it the way he is because he obviously has pretty strong feelings about it. I guess now I'm wondering if he could have anything to do with this whole nightmare."

At that, Kano stared at him. "Just because he doesn't like Reeni?" he asked in astonishment.

"No, because he was getting so volatile and angry. I read his energy. His anger rose the higher up we got to the apartment."

Damon nodded. "I have to admit I had the same thought."

"Jesus," Kano muttered. "Yet you know not a lot of people would choose to come up here right now."

"True, but it was more than that," Trevor explained. "He was getting visibly agitated and taking it out on her, as if anything that happens should be blamed on her. Blaming her is one thing, but blaming her without justification is an entirely different matter, because that also means that he's got an ax to grind in this deal."

Kano stopped, let out a slow deep breath, then grabbed his phone and called Bullard. As soon as Bullard answered, he said, "We've got a problem."

With that he put it on Speakerphone and let Damon and Trevor explain. An ugly deep silence came from the other end, as Bullard digested it. "Okay," he replied, "You all do you and let me look into Jerome. I'll get back to you."

Kano added, "But somebody needs to come here and sort it out. He exploded with way more fury than any of this warranted."

"You know that's not behavior I tolerate at any point in time," Bullard snapped. "What the hell? Kano, have you seen this kind of thing from him before?"

"No, but they're right. The higher up we got, the more nervous Jerome became. I'm not sure it has anything to do with the issue with Reeni as much as he's just incredibly uneasy about coming up here at all. Either way, he's currently not fit for duty for this assignment."

More silence came as Bullard digested that statement. "All right. I'll come see for myself." And, with that, he ended the call.

Damon smiled and nodded. "That's probably for the best, and Bullard can get to the bottom of it. Hate to cause trouble," Damon said apologetically, "but we have to call it the way we see it."

"You call it any way you want to," Kano noted. "If it's nothing to worry about, we're all good, and Jerome will learn from the experience. If it is something to worry about, I don't care who he is. I would rather find out now before somebody else gets targeted, or our home base is under attack. I've got family and friends there too," he shared.

"We're all one big family, like you guys, and keeping the predators out is always a problem." He held out a hand in peace.

"Thanks for understanding," Damon replied, shaking the man's hand. "No worries. … Let's get to work and see if we can figure out what the hell's going on at this apartment."

And, with that, Trevor gave them a nod and led them the rest of the way up into the apartment building.

CHAPTER 9

REENI SAT IN the kitchen, fidgeting with her cell phone, when Bullard walked in.

He asked her, "You want to go into town?"

She frowned. "Why?" He gave her the short explanation. She pondered that and nodded. "Sure, let's go see what's up."

"But I warn you, Jerome appears to have something against you."

"Yeah, that's nothing new," she muttered. Then she gave him half a smile. "Hey, at least maybe this time, I won't think it's both of you."

"No, I'm not against you at all," he declared, as he looked over at Dave. "We may have a situation."

Dave nodded. "Yeah, I got that. I'll keep an eye out here."

And, with that, the two of them headed into town.

As they got closer, she felt herself getting more and more tense. "Something's wrong," she whispered. "Seriously wrong."

He looked at her with a narrowed gaze. "When you say that, what do you mean?"

"I'm not sure. I'm just not sure." She shifted in her seat more and more. "Something's really wrong. I'm feeling ..." She held out her shaky hands. "Almost panicked and it's not slowing down." She frowned at him suspiciously. "You're really taking me to the apartment, right?"

Startled, he looked over at her. "Yes. Why?"

She shrugged. "Feels like my father."

"Feels like your father?" he repeated in astonishment.

"Yes, it is the same panic I feel when I'm cornered by him."

"Well, Jesus," Bullard muttered, "I haven't done anything to bring that on."

"No? What about this employee of yours? Jerome?"

He stared at her and then swore. "I have no idea," he declared in an explosive tone. "I wouldn't have thought so, but I don't know."

"All I can tell you is that, right about now, I'm getting the heebie-jeebies."

"Do you want me to turn around?" he asked instantly. "I don't want to put you in that position."

"No, no," she countered. "I don't want to leave Trevor in the lurch. Plus, if something is going on there, I don't want anything to go wrong." She wrapped her arms around her chest, feeling almost a pain inside. "I don't know what this is," she muttered. "It feels very protective, though."

"Okay, maybe you could explain that, since protective is the opposite of panicked," he pointed out, with a note of humor. "Like dumb it down a bit, as if you're talking to someone who doesn't get all this stuff."

"I'm not sure I get any of this stuff either," she acknowledged, "but it feels as if my body is curling into a ball to protect against something that's coming, and the only thing I can think of is my father."

"What about this young man, Jerome, who apparently has something against you for the type of work you do? Has he done something?"

"Yeah, but it's not even about what I do," she muttered, and then shrugged. "I have no way of knowing what he did. All I can do is tell you what I'm struggling with right now. Sometimes I think Trevor is right, and I would be better off with Terk, so maybe he could help me deal with some of this."

"I would agree with that," Bullard stated. "If you have information that can help people like me, as you did," he said with emphasis, "that information is incredibly important, and we need more people like you to get it out there. But obviously it needs to be in a sustainable, safe way for you and for us," he added, with a chuckle. "I really don't want to keep repairing my gates."

She snorted. "That's a true-enough answer."

"Oh, believe me that Leia gave me her thoughts on that whole scenario as well."

Reeni burst out laughing. "Yeah, I don't imagine she takes that kind of behavior very well. She is a force to be reckoned with in her own right."

"Exactly. She sure didn't like my behavior toward you beforehand either," he admitted, with a smile. "And, yeah, she is a force. All I can tell you is that I was worried about my family, and my frustration just boiled over. You had answers, and I wanted them … desperately, and it got the better of me."

"Yeah, well, that's the whole problem with offering information. Everybody wants a whole lot more, even if we don't have it."

"Of course," he noted. "To think that answers are out there, coming via psychics, is rather startling. Then Terk is another force unto himself, and he is very well known within his own field. So, any of us who have ever dealt with him, would never question him, not for a moment. If he says jump, we're already in the air, not even asking how high, and making it the best damn jump we can. All because, if he said *jump*, there's a damn-good reason for it, and you don't even stop and ask why."

"He is like that, *huh*? Good to know."

"Yes, he is. In your case, we did stop. We did wonder. We did have a lot of questions, and maybe we lost out on some information because of that," he admitted apologetically. "All we can do at this point is try, not even backtrack, but get to where we need to be as fast as possible."

"You're almost there." She pointed at the apartment building ahead of them. "I'm just not sure what's in there, but definitely something is." She looked at him and asked, "Are you sure you don't have any enemies around here?"

"None that I know of," he replied honestly. "I have enemies, yes. You don't do my work for a lifetime without that, but none are coming to mind locally for this." He was thinking hard and fast. "I think the part that's really upsetting me is the fact that I really don't know where this is coming from. I'm assuming it's directed at me because everybody's telling me it is, but what if somebody is here and is after one of my guys? What if it's somebody who's got a problem, … not so much with me but with one of the clients I worked for?" he asked. "What if it's just a disgruntled person who sees me as a successful businessman and wants to take me down?" He looked over at her to see what she thought.

Just as she went to say something, a bolt of energy slammed into her, and she gasped, holding onto her chest.

"Jesus, what's the matter?" Bullard asked.

She couldn't get air into her chest, and it hurt so bad. "Christ," she screeched. And then, with a wave of her hand, she managed to move the energy around her system, hitting it with little electric shocks. By the time that was done, and she could breathe again, they were parked outside the apartment building.

Bullard stared at her in horror.

"I'm fine," she whispered.

He shook his head and cried out, "Nothing was *fine* about any of that. There can't be."

"There is," she stated. "I'm fine now." She took a deep breath, then looked at him and declared, "It's definitely got *Father energy* though." He winced and she nodded. "I know. Now, for you, that means that I'm a little bit more unstable, a little bit less reasonable to deal with because now I've got daddy issues to compound the other problems at hand."

"No, no, no, no," he began. "You don't get to say that about me now. What I might have thought before versus what I'm thinking now is very different. It's not that at all."

"So, what then?"

"Reeni, … listen to me. I am very concerned about our men in that building," he stated. "So, if it has something to do with your father, that's one thing. Can you tell me if our men are safe?"

She warmed immediately at his ability to compartmentalize the issue. She looked up at the building and around the parking lot. "They're fine, but definitely something is wrong down here. I just don't know what it is."

"When you say *down here*, what do you mean?"

"*Here*-here, as in this parking lot," she replied. "I hate to say it, but it feels very much as if somebody has contacted my father, and he's here." And, with that, she hopped out and slowly walked up to the entrance of the apartment building, leaving herself fully open for any kind of an attack, if one was to come. It was the only way she knew to operate. If the attack came, then she would know she was right. If it didn't come, well then, maybe, just maybe, she'd been wrong. Unfortunately she didn't think so.

TREVOR WALKED INTO the apartment and stilled. He looked around at Damon, who nodded.

"Yeah, I feel it too."

Kano stared at them, from one to the other. "What is it you're feeling?" he asked cautiously. "And should I be alarmed?"

"Somebody has been in here, and not just law enforcement," Trevor stated, "and yet something is fairly familiar about this energy."

"When you say, fairly familiar, what do you mean?"

He shrugged. "That I can't tell you yet. If we're lucky, by the end of this visit, we'll figure it out."

"When you say *familiar*, are you saying ..." He hesitated, as Damon lifted a hand.

"Give us a chance to work for a bit," he shared, "and then we'll tell you what we come up with."

Kano snapped his jaw shut and nodded. "Hurry up," he growled.

Damon smiled at him. "We will."

Kano's tone was harsh, but neither of them took offense, because in these stressful situations, everything counted, especially time. As Damon wandered around, doing his own thing, Trevor sent his energy soaring up and above to look down. Everything that he saw as he walked through the apartment was that something in progress had been interrupted. Thank God for that, and apparently the dangerous materials had been removed, but nobody had been in to do the final checks yet. That was coming this afternoon.

So they were here first. Hopefully they could come up with something. Trevor followed his instincts and ended up in one of the two bedrooms. Damon had gone into the other. Trevor stopped in the middle of this bedroom, closed his eyes, and sent out an energy probe, looking to see what and who was here or had been here. He knew Kano was just watching, standing there, waiting for somebody to say something to him. Trevor ignored him and searched for something foreign.

It was such a faint energy that he almost missed it. He went deeper, and, when it became something strong enough that he could pick it up, he walked a little bit closer and opened up the night table drawer. Nothing was there, but he knew something was somewhere. He looked over at Kano. "Give me a hand, will you?"

They quickly flipped the mattress and, in between the mattress and the box spring, was an envelope. He pulled it out with a smile. "This is what we're after."

"Seriously?"

Trevor nodded. "Yeah, I think so."

At that, Damon came into the room, took one look, and muttered, "There it is. I saw a bed but I went to the wrong room."

"Yeah, and I went by energy, and this is what we've got." He looked around and nodded. "I think we can leave now." He looked back at Damon for confirmation.

He nodded. "Yeah, and we need to leave right away.

Something's happening." He frowned. "I don't like it, but it's outside."

And, with that, they quickly left the apartment, Trevor stuffing the envelope underneath his shirt, tucked into his pants now. As they got to the elevator, Damon sighed. "As much as I don't like it, this will be much faster." They piled into the elevator and dropped down to the ground floor.

As they stepped out, Jerome stood there, a smirk on his face. Bullard stood nearby, glaring at him, and Reeni was beside Bullard, almost cowering, while another man yelled into her face.

Trevor immediately walked over to Reeni, wrapped an arm around her shoulders, and pulled her close. He glared at the other man, who was burning like an inferno. "What the hell do you think you're doing?"

Reeni whispered, "It's my father."

He glared at the other man. "Haven't you done enough to ruin her life? Why are you here again, still trying to make her miserable?

Her father stiffened and glared at him. "I don't know you, but you are a piece of shit. I don't care if she is sleeping with you. What right do you have to talk to me like that? You can bet I'll ensure you don't have a job when this is over."

Only by accident did Trevor catch sight of Jerome's face. Trevor motioned to Damon, who gazed over at Bullard's employee. He walked closer and asked, "This is your doing, I presume?"

The smile left Jerome's face. "I don't know what you're talking about." He sneered. "She's a loose cannon for Christ's sake, so why the hell does anybody care?"

Just then her father grabbed her by the arm and pulled

her out of Trevor's arms and toward the waiting car. She cried out in pain, and he glared at her. "God, you're such a whiner," he declared in the same disgusted tone. "I can't wait to get you locked up where you belong."

"That's not happening," Trevor snapped, his tone hard. "You don't have any rights here."

"Of course, I do. I don't give a rat's ass about this fucking country. And nobody here will stop me from taking my runaway daughter home."

Trevor shook his head. "Your daughter is an adult. She has a right to choose what she wants and where she wants to go. She can stay where she is."

"Not according to the paperwork I have," he declared, with a sneer. "I got that all locked down a long time ago, and nothing anybody can do about it."

He was nothing if not arrogant.

"She's mine to do with as I will, and that's how it'll be. I'll ensure she can't get away this time." He glared at her. "You're such an embarrassment. You're a fucking nightmare, just like your sister."

"What happened to my sister?" she asked, stopping in her tracks, turning to face him. "Outside of the fact that you probably locked her up too."

"Of course I did, and her husband was fully agreeable. He wanted a decent wife, and I couldn't hold him to the marriage, not after I realized she was trying to divorce him," he replied, with a groan. "After everything I've done for you ungrateful little whiners, that's what you do."

"What? You mean choose to live with somebody we care about instead of being an object to be abused by you?" Reeni replied, defiance in her tone. That response had everybody turning to look at her. "You've done nothing but manipulate us, steal from us, lie and connive everyone with your crooked lawyers to take away our inheritance, when all you care about is making sure we do what you want us to do. Even Mom's locked up, isn't she? You somehow got her sectioned too."

"Your mother is unstable," he declared in a very gentle tone now. "I get that you're the same, and you just don't understand, but that's all right. I'll ensure the doctors take good care of you."

"Like hell," she roared, as she stepped back and glared at him. "No way I'm going anywhere with you. Not now, not ever."

"That's too bad you feel that way, but you can't stop me."

"Really?" she asked, her anger flaring.

Trevor smiled. There was the woman he knew. Strong, confident, still learning to burn.

Reeni continued. "What you're doing right now is completely illegal and the African government, whether they like it or not, is supposed to save me from assholes like you. Then you can go through the proper channels to try and extradite me out of here," she explained. "However, I'm not going without a major screaming fit happening right here and right now. Believe me that *this time* is like nothing you have ever seen before."

He looked over at the rest of the men, standing beside Reeni, now glaring at him too. "No, *you* don't understand," he noted in a calm tone. "She's a danger to herself and to everybody else around her," he explained, trying damn hard to convince everyone. "She needs help, professional medical help."

Bullard stepped forward, obviously furious. "You're right about one thing. She needs help, but not in the form of you.

She needs somebody to save her from you," he stated, his tone hard. "We don't abuse women here."

Her father laughed. "This is Africa. Of course you do. Women are no better, no worse than anybody who can take advantage of them," he snapped, with a sneer. "I don't know who the hell she's got as a protector in you, but you're nobody, and, by the time I'm done with you, if you even think to interfere, you won't be anybody."

Bullard stared at him, and a slow smile crossed his face. "Challenge accepted," he declared. "I don't think you have any idea who you've just tried to take on."

At that, the other guy with Reeni's father looked around uneasily. "My name is Matthew Cantor," he announced, "just in case you need it for the record."

"I already know your name," Bullard stated, with a wry smile that was just a bit unsettling. "I already know everything I need to know. Right now, your wife is filing divorce papers, and the cops are looking to bring you up on criminal charges, even as we speak."

Reeni turned and looked at Bullard in shock. "What?"

He nodded. "The doctor who has been signing all this bogus paperwork passed away, and his son took over the business. So he is doing what he can to rectify the criminal activities his father engaged in for profit, one of which was signing documents to commit your mother, your sister, and yourself, as your father saw fit," Bullard shared with one and all. "Completely illegally, but it allowed him to control your fortune, which by the way is quite vast. Here you are, trying hard to stay afloat, yet he's been controlling your money all this time."

Her father stepped back and glared at Bullard. "I don't know who are you or what you think you are doing," he bellowed, "but you won't interfere in my family business."

"I've already stopped it. It didn't take much, just a couple phone calls to set things in motion. Also, you have a slight issue regarding tax evasion, and it seems the US Treasury is looking into your history pretty intently at the moment. Then we also have the other nuisances of the criminal charges for what you've done to your wife and daughters, including Reeni. That involves you too, Matthew."

Matthew stiffened and glared at him. "I haven't done anything wrong," he stated. "It's obvious that they're desperately in need of help. Have you listened to the crap that comes out of her mouth?"

Bullard nodded. "Yeah, and I wish I'd listened earlier to some of it," he admitted. "But I didn't, so that's my mistake. I won't make a second one, by letting you haul her away as if she's damaged goods. That won't happen."

"You can't stop us," her father roared, as he grabbed her by the arm and jerked her hard toward the car.

She jerked back, pulling her arm free again. "I won't get hauled out of here just because you say so," she cried out. "I've been looking for a lawyer myself to fight you."

"That's not happening," he thundered. "I have documents that say how inept and totally unequipped you are to handle life in this world. So, believe me that the judge will listen to that over anything you have to say," he argued, with a sneer.

"Not necessarily," Bullard snapped, "particularly when it was all obtained illegally and for the purpose of controlling her money."

"I don't need her money," he snapped. "I have more than enough for my own needs."

"If that's the case, it's interesting that you decided that you had to have hers anyway," Damon noted, stepping closer to Reeni. "Because you're the one who's been handling it all this time."

"I had no choice," he stated. "These things have to be managed. It's a father's sacrifice." He spoke in such a woebegone patronizing tone of voice that everybody stiffened and glared at him. "Look, this is a private family issue. It's got nothing to do with any of you." He motioned at Trevor. "You can find somebody else to sleep with, one who won't be waking you up with night terrors," he pointed out, with an eyeroll.

"Is that what it is to you?" Trevor asked. "Somebody who has deep-seated nightmares of being held captive, kidnapped in the middle of night by her own father, and locked away in institutions? That's all it is to you? ... Something to mock, something to make fun of, just because you can?"

Her father glared at her. "I'm not the source of her night terrors," he declared. "Even my mother had the same strain of mental instability. I know what I'm talking about, and you guys obviously don't. Somehow Tangerine has managed to show you a different side of her."

"No, I haven't," she argued. "They have seen the exact same side as you have, but they're not terrified by it, like you are." She pointed at him. "That says something."

"It doesn't say anything," he countered, with yet another sneer. "You don't scare me, but you can bet I'll ensure you're locked up so that you don't scare the rest of the world either."

"Of course. That's what you do with everybody you can't control," she replied. She glanced back at the driver.

"So, did he just hire you from here, or did you come with him?"

The driver looked at her in confusion. "I was ordered to pick him up at the airport and to bring the two of you back to the airport," he said. "I've never worked with him before."

"In that case," she began, "you may want to just take off because it's likely to get a little uglier here, and people might think you're involved."

At that, his eyebrows shot up. "You really don't want to go?"

"Hell no," she spat, "I have no intention of going anywhere with this man. He's a deranged power-hungry kidnapper," she shared, "a bully, who likes to play games with people for his own entertainment."

And, with that, the driver tilted his head toward her. "Good luck." He quickly drove off, leaving her father stranded.

"Now what will you do?" she asked, with a laugh. "It's not as if you can just drag me through town at will. Not everybody here wants to be part of your crooked little operation," she muttered. "I would be very, very happy if the taxman showed up. I've also got information for him that he would love."

"You don't have anything," he scoffed.

"Oh, actually I do. I got it from Grandma," she stated, with a smile. "She wanted to ensure that you could never treat the rest of us like you treated her, so she'd been compiling information for a very long time," she explained. "I just didn't have anybody in my corner I could trust with this information to help put you away."

He stared at her in shock, and she nodded. "Yeah, so you should be making plans yourself right now, because, whether you leave me alone or not," she promised, with a sneer of her own this time, "we're coming after you. We'll be around to confirm that you get to spend the rest of your life, not in a nice padded little cell like you arranged for your family, but in prison, where you can deal with criminals, some who may not take kindly to you locking up your entire family so you could control their inheritance." She smiled as she added, "Not everybody likes abusers."

He looked uncomfortable for a moment and then scoffed. "You're just making empty threats. Crazy little bitch."

"Oh, not empty threats," she confirmed. "I do have that information. I've been looking for an honest person to go to bat for me, a lawyer, somebody I could trust, but trust is something that's a little thin on the ground these days. Particularly when it comes to this because almost everybody can be bought off, as you have found out quite easily. You've had to buy a lot of them."

"I bought off your last attorney," he stated, with that endless sneer.

"Which is why I didn't try again because I couldn't tell who to trust," she admitted. "However, now I've found some trustworthy people, who can't be bought by you."

"I doubt it," he muttered. "I can offer them a million bucks each, and believe me that every one of them will take it."

Bullard just shook his head. "No, I sure can't be bothered for that paltry sum," he replied, with a cheerful smile. "You want to talk billions, and I might be interested, but probably not, because I just don't like you," he proclaimed in an ugly tone. "I've had quite enough out of you. I know exactly what kind of a guy you are. I've spent a lifetime fighting assholes like you, and believe me that you are not taking her away, and we will definitely be coming after you."

With that, Bullard pulled out his phone and called back the driver. When he showed up, Bullard ordered, "Take him to the airport and ensure he gets on his plane."

At that, the driver grinned. "Absolutely." He led her father to the car.

Her father turned to her and vowed, "This isn't the end of it. My team is here. I might leave, but they will stay to deal with you."

"No, it isn't the end," she agreed, "because the tide has turned, and I'm coming after you now." She smiled. "That you can believe, and I will make you pay for what you did to the rest of my family. Once my sister and my mother realize they really are safe, I'll ensure they testify about what you've done to them. It's over. We've had enough of you and everything you've done to us. See you later, *Dad.*"

At that point, he was shoved into the car, and they drove off.

She turned to Bullard and studied him for a moment. "Did you mean it, or was that all a bluff?"

"I meant it." He nodded. "You don't know me that well yet, and what you do know probably isn't all that positive," he added, with a smile. "Yet I meant every word. I don't say what I don't mean, and your father needs somebody in a position of power to stop him."

"True."

"Believe me that I have that power, and between me and the rest of the team, we know a lot of people in this world who will go to bat for you," he shared. "So, yes, I can't say your problems are over, and, in many ways, they're just starting, but your father or his minions won't lock you up ever again."

"So, you say, but, if I get kidnapped in a dark alley, with nobody around, he's still got all that paperwork, doesn't he?"

Bullard nodded. "That he does, at least until we can get some of this sorted out," he admitted. "It shouldn't take long, but it will take a day or two more," he muttered. "So, we need you to stay safe in the meantime."

"Yeah, well, in order to do that," she stated, "I'm definitely leaving your place."

Bullard glared at her, but she pointed toward Jerome. "He's the one who called my father. Jerome is the one willing to turn me in as a sacrificial goat. For money I'm sure, but also because I made him very uncomfortable, and he was upset that you were foolish enough to listen to me. So, while I do feel more welcome there, I'm still not sure I'm safe at your place."

Bullard turned to Jerome, who glared at the group. "I can't believe you're listening to her. It's obvious that she's got serious problems. Why didn't you just let her father take her away?"

"Why would we?" Damon asked, studying him. "We don't do that to people."

"She needs help, so you should look at it from that point of view," Jerome snapped. "It's obvious that people need to be helped, and she couldn't help herself, so somebody had to step up and do what was right." He sneered at Kano. "Even you were smitten. Somebody just has to say a few little things, and suddenly everybody here is all gaga about her. It's all bullshit."

With a flick of Bullard's hand, Damon and Kano secured Jerome, including cuffing his hands and his feet. When he started to loudly object, they obliged him with a gag in his mouth.

She stared over at Damon and then back at Trevor. "That confirms how my father found me," she stated, "but it doesn't answer the question about what you found."

Trevor nodded. "We did find some things," he murmured. "It might answer some other questions as well, but it would be nice if we could get out of the public eye, preferably before the cops come and start tearing apart that place."

Bullard narrowed his gaze at him. "Did you guys find something?"

Trevor nodded. "So, can we get back to your place and maybe sort it out there?"

He nodded. "We will, indeed. Let's go." And, with that, they all quickly trooped back to Bullard's compound, with some adjustments. Bullard took Jerome and Damon and Kano back with him. That left Trevor driving Reeni with him.

On the drive over, Trevor kept his hand on her the whole time. She shifted against him and whispered, "I'm fine, you know?"

He grinned at her. "You're more than fine. You handled that great. You didn't succumb to the fear, and you did really, really well," he stated warmly.

She sighed and snuggled in close. "I'm sorry for all my father's insults—to you, I mean."

He looked at her and then laughed. "Honey, those were hardly even insults. They were just an old man scared of losing control."

"Yep, that's what he is, but he will lose control," she declared in a determined tone.

"He will. Whether he knows it or not, he has a whole new reality coming his way."

"Maybe we shouldn't have warned him though," she murmured. "He'll just have a chance to pull his forces together and to make our lives even more difficult. He might even hide away."

"That's fine if he does," he replied, reassuring her. "Bullard meant it. He's contacted people, and I know Terk has as well."

"Sure, but *contacting people*," she repeated, using her fingers to make air quotes, "doesn't mean that those people will act or will be willing to help."

"Terk and Bullard both have a whole lot of *people*," he noted, with a grin on his face, "people at their beck and call, who are more than willing to help out, particularly when it's something that's so obviously injurious to you."

She shook her head. "I hope so. The thought of my sister and my mother both being locked up, knowing there's no chance he would ever let them out, really makes me want to cry."

"Don't bother crying," Trevor suggested. "We will get you back over there, and you can say hello to them in person."

She smiled. "Now that would be nice."

"I presume you do have some kind of a relationship with them then."

"If my father's out of the way, I might," she said, thinking back. "My mother always seemed to be his malleable instrument, so I'm not too sure what there is for a relationship between us."

"But remember that she's also taken a lot more years of his abuse than you have."

"Right, and I do need to consider that." She sighed. "I would like to think she's a good person. No," she corrected in a firmer tone. "I choose to believe it."

"If she has been under his thumb all this time, it couldn't have been easy on her."

"No, it wouldn't have been easy at all," she agreed. She then smiled and nodded. "I guess it's a good thing I came over here after all. It was a good decision."

"Absolutely," Trevor confirmed. "Now we need to resolve the problem at Bullard's place."

She pondered that, and he studied her face, waiting to see how she would handle that. "Even though Jerome must also be involved in that mess, I guess it's all about learning to trust the rest of Bullard's men, isn't it?"

"It is," he said. "An awful lot in life comes to us if we just give it a chance to find us. Now your father created all kinds of trouble and trauma and your innate need to stay out of the middle of all this mess. So those issues just confuse the process." He grabbed her hand and gently squeezed it. "By the way, I'm really proud of the way you handled yourself there."

She snorted. "All I did was shriek and scream at him."

"Exactly." He chuckled. "You stood up to a bully. You fought back, physically and verbally. You did very well. Considering what you've been through and what he intended to do"—he beamed at her—"you did really well."

She leaned back, looked up at him, and smiled. "There's that cheerleader again."

He rolled his eyes. "Don't say that," he scolded softly.

She scooted over closer to him.

"What do you think we'll find at Bullard's place?" he murmured.

"The answers," she muttered, followed by a yawn. "I have to admit that I've been off my game. Maybe not even so much off my game, but more like … I'm just seeing more clearly now."

"I think that, once the fear gets out of your system, a lot more can fall into place."

"You're right there," she stated. "And it definitely has a weird electrical sense." She pondered that. "I also don't know why."

"Why is a part of it, and something for us to figure out at the same time," he noted. "When this is over, will you consider coming back to England and spending some time with me?"

She smiled at him and nodded. "I would like that. I just have to deal with my family first and ensure they're okay."

"You do," he agreed, with a nod. "But nobody said you had to deal with it alone." She looked at him for a long moment, and he saw tears come to her eyes. He smiled, then gave her a quick kiss, and whispered, "I mean that."

As they pulled into the gates at Bullard's place, which opened automatically, she sighed. "I wonder if I will ever look at these gates in the same way."

"Probably not, but then again," Trevor added, with a laugh, "neither will Bullard."

As they all exited their vehicles in front of the compound, Bullard pointed at the front gates, then turned to Reeni and grinned. "Even an old dog needs to be taught new tricks every once in a while," he admitted.

She smiled at him. "Thanks for your help back there with my father."

He shrugged. "Your father's an asshole," he declared cheerfully. "We'll have some fun bringing him down a peg or two."

"Needs to be more than a peg or two," she stated. "Otherwise my life will never be the same."

"Okay. I'll be happy to make it a big peg or two then," he clarified, still chuckling. "But table that for the moment, because I need your help here."

She nodded. "Even if you don't like what I see, what I tell you?"

His eyebrows shot up, and he stared at her intently. "Especially if I don't like it." He looked over at Trevor, who just shrugged. "I'm just grounding for her," he shared. "Yet she seems to think something is happening."

"Good that we're back then," Bullard muttered.

As they walked into the main room, several of the staff came out to greet them. Trevor nodded and explained, "We found an envelope at the apartment, and we need to sort out its contents. We haven't seen them yet, but the choice was made to come back here, where we would have the privacy to sort it out."

"That makes sense," Dave agreed. "Let's take a look." And he pointed over at the dining room table.

Just as they got to the table, the lights flickered.

Reeni looked back at Trevor. "Here we go again, but how and why?" She looked over at Dave. "Do you have any pets here?" she asked.

He frowned at her. "There's always been cats around, although we've lost a few lately." He added, "We're not exactly sure what happened to one in particular, but he's gone missing. I keep calling for him and putting out food for him, but I have seen no sign of the cat."

She nodded, as she looked back at Damon. "Any chance you can track a cat?"

He frowned at her. "Can't say I've tried. Is it important?"

"Yeah, it is." She faced Dave now. "You really liked that cat too, didn't you?"

He nodded. "I do. Two of them were older, and, when they disappeared, I more or less expected it. A lot of times, animals just choose to disappear and hole up someplace to die," he noted, "but this particular cat was young, smart, and a favorite of mine." He looked at her hopefully. "Are you saying that you can find him?" He looked over at Damon. "Can you?" Then he turned back to Reeni. "Can he?"

"Honestly, I'm not sure," Damon admitted. "I've never been asked to track a cat before."

"I'm asking now," she clarified, turning to him. "And it's important."

An audible snort of disgust came from the other side of the room.

She turned and glared at Jerome, noting he was no longer handcuffed, and his gag had been removed. "That's enough out of you," she snapped. "I don't have to take insults from you."

He glared back at her. "I don't have to take this shit either."

"That's a good start," she said. "Why don't you quit then?"

He stared at her in astonishment. "Why the hell should I quit? I've always wanted to be here."

"What do you mean, you *always* wanted to be here?"

"I always wanted to be here. This is where I belong," he declared, glaring at her. "You don't."

There was an uncomfortable shuffling around her as the others realized some personality issue was going on.

She shrugged and looked over at Bullard. "I don't know what you want to do."

Bullard studied her for a moment and replied, "Maybe you could give me a hint."

She frowned, and, without saying anything else to Bullard, she turned to Damon. "I really need that cat."

"Fine, give me a minute." And, with that, he left the room.

She nodded, and as Jerome stood, she added in a caustic tone, "I would like you to stay here."

"I don't care what you want," he stated, with a hard glare. "The last thing I need is to have some crazy chick like you ordering me around." And, with that, he quickly made his escape.

She turned to Trevor and nodded.

His eyebrows shot up, and he studied her.

CHAPTER 10

REENI WHISPERED, "PLEASE follow Jerome."

Without another word, Trevor turned and disappeared.

"What the hell is going on?" Leia asked, as she looked from one to the other. "I gather that we've come up against somebody who doesn't like psychics?"

"That's part of it, yes," Reeni agreed, "and the other part is just way too simple."

At that, Bullard glared at her. "If it's so damn simple, stop jerking me around and explain it."

She sighed. "I could, but I really do need the cat."

"What if you can't get the cat?" he asked in frustration.

"Oh, we can get the cat," she stated. "That's not really the problem."

He just stared at her and shook his head. "It would be a whole lot easier if you could make some sense, and right now, but you're not."

"You know," she began, immediately speaking in a mocking tone, "it would be a whole lot easier if you had a *leettle* bit of patience right now, yet you don't."

Her intentional mispronunciation of the word, combined with the surprised look on Bullard's face, had Leia chortling with laughter. "Oh, my goodness, I love this."

Bullard turned to frown at his wife. "How can you possibly love this?" he cried out in an faux-injured tone.

"You do need a talking to sometimes," she pointed out. "So, if this is the form that you choose to have it happen, that's fine with me."

He just stared at his wife in bemusement, then turned back to Reeni. "So, is this misguided payback for all your pent-up anger at all the kids who gave you hell over that red hair of yours? Because I had nothing to do with that."

"Jesus, did they ever give me hell," she agreed, with a chuckle. "It still gives me nothing but hell sometimes," she added in a cheerful tone. "But that's okay, as most of the time it doesn't bother me at all. But, every once in a while though, people get a one-two shot, and I pay the price, but most of the time I'm good."

He nodded. "Having a temper can be a challenge."

"It can be a great challenge," she confirmed. "Sometimes to control it, and sometimes to let it loose. I hadn't realized just how much my father was inhibiting everything I do. But now? … It feels very different, so it'll take me a little bit to sort some of that out," she noted apologetically, staring at him. "So, when you ask for answers, just know that I'm dealing with a different deck of cards right now."

He nodded in understanding. "So much of this is emotion and intuition, isn't it?"

"It's all of that and more," she declared. "Apparently, when I put up all the fear barriers to keep my father away, I was shutting down other avenues to an extent that I'm not even aware of at this point," she admitted. "So it's, … it's a little hard for me to pull out of it right away."

"Take your time, and do what you need to do," Leia stated comfortably.

Reeni grinned at her. "I'm working on it. Bullard's not

terribly happy with my lack of progress or my lack of speed, but I am sure he will be pretty cheerful soon."

"That depends," Bullard said, staring at her. "It depends an awful lot on what you'll say."

And that wiped the smile off her face. "Yeah, that's the part I can't control, so that's over to you."

"And again we're talking in circles," he muttered.

She smiled. "I wouldn't say circles, but it's not clear just yet. All I need is Damon and Trevor to return."

Just then Damon walked in, carrying a huge cat. She stared at it and muttered, "Good God, is that a bobcat or something?"

"No, it's a Manx," Dave exclaimed, rushing forward and picking up the big thing as if it were a baby. He buried his face in its fur and sighed happily.

"Yeah, well, you might want to look for something a little extra though," she suggested.

Dave lifted his head and frowned at her. "Pardon?"

"Take a closer look. Does he have a collar?"

"No, I never put a collar on him," he stated, not really understanding her question. So he looked to show her, then realized that a collar was on the cat's neck. Dave's facial expression turned hard.

"Jesus," Bullard muttered. "What is it?"

"You know those electronic devices used at some museums, to track when a painting is moved?"

Bullard frowned. "Those RFID tags or the like, to track a stolen painting?"

"Basically that, but tweaked by a hacker," Reeni said. "Instead of the cat's special collar sending an alarm that a painting was stolen, it is sending some signal to cut off your lights, internet, satellite, depending on what room the cat is in, or something like that. I don't understand how that works. Your team can figure that out. Now the cat did not do this by choice, mind you, so you really can't shoot the messenger," she rushed to say, making sure they didn't take it out on her or on the poor cat.

"So, as much as you don't want to hear this, what's going on here is literally an inside job. A lot of it has been done by this furry guy, resulting in the electrical outages. However, the rest of it, like the changes made to the outside box, needed somebody else's help. And it's connected somehow to our bomb-maker in town, though I'm not exactly sure yet. I was hoping you guys could make some connection there. It's related to Bullard somehow," she stated, with a shrug.

Bullard stared at her, his face working, as he realized it would be somebody on his own team. He looked around at everybody gathered here, as they all understood the implications of what Reeni said.

She looked over at Damon. "You know it'll just look bad if I say it."

He nodded. He faced Bullard, and in an understanding tone, added, "It explains the behavior."

Bullard groaned. "We're talking about Jerome, aren't we?"

She nodded. "At least in part. I don't know whether he's being paid to do it, or if this is an experiment. I'm really not sure at all," she said apologetically. "That part's not coming through very clearly right now, but, as I said, I'm dealing with some technical issues," she offered, with a grin.

Bullard turned to Dave, who nodded. "We'll go get him."

Someone interrupted, "No, you won't."

They all turned just in time to see Jerome stepping into

the kitchen, holding an automatic rifle.

Reeni caught a glimpse of Trevor behind Jerome. Probably others saw Trevor there too. Just not Jerome.

"What are you doing with that?" Bullard snapped.

"Her," Jerome replied, "it's her."

"What's her?"

"She's the problem. You need to get rid of her. If it wasn't for her, you would never even be questioning me."

Bullard stared at him. "If you didn't have anything to do with it, why are you standing there, holding that weapon?"

"Because it's the only way I'll get you to listen," he replied.

Bullard stopped and stared. "You want me to listen?"

"Yeah, I want you to listen. You never listen to me, never. Ever since I started working here. I told you how I could do so much more, but you wouldn't listen."

"And I told you that you needed to understand how things worked around here before you could step up and do more," Bullard retorted, glaring at him. "Violence and threats and sabotage aren't the way to get a promotion in life."

"Obviously because of *her* I won't get a promotion now," he grumbled, as he shifted the weapon on his arm.

Reeni realized just how ugly a position they were in, including Leia, who even now was looking with shock at this man she had welcomed into her home. Reeni asked him, "You tried really hard to get to work here for a long time, didn't you?"

"Yes, only because Bullard finally had a need, with so many jobs to do and with some of his men busy with family obligations," he explained, with an eyeroll, "so I managed to get the job. And that was a very lucky coincidence since I happened to be in the right place at the right time," he added, with a smirk. "Yet they don't really appreciate me. None of them do."

Leia nodded. "Meaning that you can do so much more, but they wouldn't give you that chance?"

"Of course," he agreed, with a shrug. "I worked here for months now, but nobody would talk to me, nobody would let me do things, nobody would let me into that seat of power," he complained, "and that's where I belong."

Bullard appeared to be shocked.

"See? You don't even know who I am. You don't know anything about me," Jerome complained, staring at Bullard. "That's because you didn't care, and then this little strumpet comes along."

Reeni stiffened at the phrase and glared at him.

Jerome sneered at her. "Then she makes a couple little woo-woo things happen, and the next thing you know, you guys are falling all over her. I'm not so stupid or gullible."

"You are definitely somebody who can be bought," Reeni stated.

He looked at her. "I didn't know they had these plans," he said. "It's not as if anything was inherently wrong with what they asked of me. They just wanted me to put something on the damn cat. I'm not stupid or anything, but I obviously knew that we were heading for a problem, but I figured, if I rescued everybody here from the group's plans, then all of you would finally see me for what I could do."

Reeni stared at Jerome. "Some gang talked you into doing their dirty work, didn't they? This was just a test, wasn't it? That's why it felt so wrong. It wasn't even necessarily a real attack, but it was all about you getting a chance to be the big man, the big hero, while placating the gang that owns you."

"Except that I didn't get the chance, did I?" he snapped, staring at her. "You came along and ruined everything."

"Yeah, blame me," she said in a hard tone. "Let's completely ignore the fact that you set this all up, let this sabotage happen. But some gang was supposed to help you, right?"

"Well, yeah. They were supposed to help me show Bullard how I could do so much more. I talked to a few friends, and they talked to a few friends, and we came up with this idea. We would set off all the electrical at the compound, have things shut down randomly, setting up some really interesting scenarios. Then I would come along and would solve it all."

"When would you do that?" she asked. "You had plenty of time to be the hero, long before I got here."

"I could have done it any time, except that you came to the front door, without any warning, and told him that something funky was going on in his house, and then everything started to shift," he complained. "I didn't even get a chance to show him how I could fix it."

"You never made any attempt either, did you?"

"No, because I was trying to offset you," he snapped, glaring at her. "What the hell was that all about? Who walks up to somebody's goddamn gated compound, especially somebody like Bullard, and tells him that he's got a problem in his own house for crying out loud," he cried out. "None of us. I even talked to the guys, and nobody had any idea who you were or what you were up to. Nobody could even begin to see that you would be a problem. Sure enough, right out of the blue one day, you show up with this cock-and-bull story about somebody having a problem with his electronics.

And, sure enough, that's exactly what we were doing, but not to hurt anybody," he added, growling at her. "Just to show Bullard that I could do more, that I could step up and fix things."

"Oh, yeah. You broke it so you could fix it, supposedly, yet you never stopped the sabotage." She stared at him. "Now look at you. You're standing there with a weapon in your hand, trying to tell Bullard that you're some specialist who could do so much more. Instead you have just proven yourself to be a bully, a mercenary, a man with only violence as his trade in life. Do you really think Bullard will let you loose with anything right now?"

Jerome glared at her. "All I ever wanted was to work for Bullard. He was somebody in the industry with a big name, and I wanted that respectability," he explained in frustration, then turned to Bullard. "The whole mercenary thing was getting to be a bit much, and I needed out. So, when I got hired here, it was perfect. However, very quickly I realized Bullard had me pigeonholed as this trainee, and you would never give me a chance to get out of that beginner's slot."

Bullard, to give him credit, still stared at Jerome, half in shock, Reeni suspected, but Jerome's words rang true. "I see, so, when I came along I just ruined all your plans."

Jerome nodded. "Honestly, I didn't realize it, but the people I was working with on the side had plans of their own."

"Oh, so was that all their lovely bomb-making equipment we found?"

He nodded. "I didn't know anything about that," he declared. "That's not on me."

"But you were part of it," she declared, "so it is on you."

"No, it's not," he repeated, pulling back the lever on the

gun and pointing it in her direction. "It's not."

She stared at him, wondering what it would take for him to realize the situation he was in. "At least nobody got killed. At least in this scenario, everyone is still standing, and no one was killed. But if the gang finds out that we know about you and your participation in all this, it could get ugly. Of course, if you would have helped the police, things would be different now."

He stared at her in shock. "Are you nuts? The gang would kill me."

She nodded. "And when your gang buddies find out that you're no longer doing this *with* them, don't you think they'll have something to say about that too?"

He swallowed and shrugged. "They know I'm with them."

"You're a mercenary," she declared, her tone caustic. "I'm pretty sure they know that you're out for the highest bidder. You helped them—no, scratch that—you *paid* them, didn't you?"

"Oh, I didn't pay them much. I needed some help though. They had to make the devices. I've got one device like the one on the cat too," he shared. "It's just something I can attach to my watch, and then I can set things on and off as I need to. That's how I took over the power box outside on the street. They gave me another device to set it off. They're harmless though."

"Harmless, "she repeated. "Hundreds of thousands of dollars of city damage, the worry, the stress. Harmless? Where in all of this was your rescue?" she cried out. "There's no rescue to be had here. All you did was make things worse because you wanted to be in control, because you like to play games."

He glared at her. "Who do you think you are?" he roared. "I was just showing Bullard that I could do more. So much more."

"And you did do more, more sabotage. You showed him how you could mess up the electrical here, even the satellite, but who's to say that Bullard will want anything to do with you now?" she asked. "Your methodology is definitely not in line with who and what Bullard is."

"What do you know or care?" Jerome asked, staring at her. "You sure as hell don't know anything about his code."

"Sure I do," she argued, "especially after I did some soul-searching once Bullard and I had our little gate incident, but none of that has anything to do with you and why you're here creating such chaos. You'll have to explain this to an awful lot of people."

"I don't have to explain anything to anybody," he declared. "Nobody knows that I was involved with that gang at the apartment building."

"That's why you kept complaining about me, the closer you got to the upstairs apartment, isn't it?" she asked. "Because you knew that, if any of your bomb-making buddies were there, they could easily finger you or could see that you had fingered them."

"I shouldn't have been anywhere close to that apartment," he stated, with a shudder. "Those guys don't fool around."

"No, they sure don't, and that's why you'll tell us who they are."

"No, I will not," he stated, with a headshake. "I absolutely will not."

She looked over at Damon and Trevor. "Surely one of you guys is getting something."

"Yep, I am," Trevor confirmed, looking at the angry young man. "I'm getting a Marta and a Josiah."

At that, Jerome's face paled. "What? No way. How the fuck—"

"Yeah, don't worry. We'll be sure to let the police know that you cooperated," Reeni quipped, with half a smile. "At least as far as sharing their names."

"No, no, no, no, no, you don't understand," he muttered, staring at her in horror. "I'm not kidding. These guys will kill me."

"How was it that you managed to be a mercenary?" she asked curiously. "You're obviously scared of these guys."

"I'm not scared," he stated, "respectful maybe. But they made it very clear that, if I wanted what I wanted, and if they helped, then I would have to shut up about their stuff. Help them from time to time."

"Did you ever get an idea of what it was they were really trying to do?"

"No, I didn't want to ask too many questions. I, ... I don't do bomb stuff," he muttered.

"You know perfectly well what is required of mercs," she snapped.

He glared at her. "But I'm not one of them. That's not ... I've been honest since I started working for Bullard here."

Reeni snorted at that. "Right, honest. Are they also the ones who cleaned your background history, who gave you your fake cover story, as some computer expert?" He looked at her, puzzled for a moment, and then she added, "So you could work here for Bullard?"

"Sure. So, when I got here, Bullard needed somebody to do basic computer work, so it wasn't hard to clean up some of the incoming information before it got any further," Jerome noted. "I was a little worried at the time, but I was hired temporarily. Then, when it turned out to be a good deal for them," he said, with a proud smile, "I was doing more and more, but then it stopped. It's as if they couldn't quite figure out what to do with me."

"There's a reason for that," Bullard declared, "and that's because I had a bad feeling about you. I may not have known your whole story, but something always felt *off.*"

"No way." Jerome glared at Bullard. "No way anything was off. This is all I ever wanted, and I played it right."

Reeni shook her head. "Yet, when you got that opportunity to *fix the sabotage, be the hero,* you blew it. Now what will you do? You might shoot all of us. You might wound half of us," she added, with a shrug, "but you sure as hell won't take us all out and go on your merry way."

"But I didn't do anything, so I can just leave."

Reeni snorted. "I don't think the cops will be too happy with that response. Plus, they need to know more about these bomb-making friends of yours."

"I'm not telling them anything," he said in a panic. "No way I'll do that, and you, … you can't make me."

Smiling, she walked closer to Jerome and smirked. "Remember those times you saw me touch things, all those electrical items?"

He brought the gun up. "Oh, I remember all right. You're some weird freak," he claimed. "I should do the world a favor and take you out first. At least then I won't have to worry about anybody else listening to you. Besides, your father was right."

She stared at him and sighed. "That's all right." She placed her hand on the gun barrel. She noted the smoothness of it. "These things aren't even wood anymore, not all metal either, are they?"

"Only the barrel," Bullard muttered behind her.

She nodded, letting her hand slip around the metal barrel. Then she jolted some electricity toward the end of it. Shocks flared off Jerome's hands, and he dropped the rifle to the ground. Immediately somebody behind her picked up the gun.

Jerome stared at her. "What the hell? What did you do to me?"

"I didn't do anything," she replied in astonishment. "What could I possibly do? I just touched your gun. I didn't do anything else." She shared a quick glance with Trevor.

"You did. You did too," he cried out, looking over at Bullard.

She touched Jerome's hand and asked, "You don't feel anything now, do you?"

Immediately he grabbed her by the neck, pulling her tight against his chest. "No, but you'll be my ticket out of here, you bitch," he muttered. "I don't like the look on any of their faces." He started to back up, pulling her with him and out of the room.

She asked Trevor, *Do I have to be nice?*

Nope, now you sure don't, Trevor said cheerfully.

Good. She reached up with both hands, grabbed Jerome's watch with one hand and his ring with the other hand and just pulsed energy between her hands. The energy surged and crackled, and Jerome cried out, as the smell of burning flesh filled the air. She shut it down and twisted to look at the man, now crying on the floor. She looked over at Trevor. "I am so sorry. Honestly, I tried to shut it off right away."

"That's okay," Trevor said, as he looked down at Jerome. "Lucky for him, Bullard can fix it."

"Not sure I will though," he declared in a hard tone. He looked at her at her and asked, "Could you always do that?"

She nodded. "Yeah, more or less."

"Damn, I guess I'm lucky it was just the gate."

She gave him a ghost of a smile. "Yes, you certainly are. I do try not to hurt people though." Then she heard the cat screech and looked over at him. "The cat really wants that damn thing off his neck. The electrical currents are not good for him at all."

Dave had it off within seconds, and the cat was soon purring, rubbing up against Dave's legs. "He'll get some salmon right now, poor little guy." And, with that, Dave and the cat went straight to the refrigerator.

Reeni looked over at the others hesitatingly.

Damon nodded. "Good skill."

"I have to have metal though," she murmured.

Damon looked down at Jerome, saw both the ring and the watch, and smiled. "People never think about jewelry, do they?"

She shrugged. "Not really, and, in this case, that's a good thing."

"It's an absolutely great thing," Damon declared, with a bright smile.

Trevor raised a hand, holding the envelope they had retrieved from the bomb-making apartment. "Now that we have Jerome, let's check out what was left behind in the bomber's apartment."

They all gathered around the kitchen table, as Dave, with his precious cat scarfing salmon beside him, stood guard over Jerome, who was still moaning and rolling on the floor.

Trevor opened the envelope and looked through the documents. He jumped to the end to find a signature. "The authorities had a mole in place, tracking this international terrorist group." With that language, Trevor met Bullard's gaze. "Seems the Josiah that Reeni mentioned was also known as Reeves."

Bullard grimaced. "Nasty bastard. His bombs killed hundreds of people. We finally traced them back to him. Then we lost him and his group. That op was my one failure."

Trevor shook his head. "Not according to this." Trevor pointed to one page and read from it. "Thanks to the intel from Bullard's group, we got one of our men inserted into the gang. Once he was accepted, we allowed the terrorist group to leave the country, to cement our inside man's position and his safety."

Trevor read on. "Bullard was known to the terrorist group and was their number one target, especially after the death of Reeves. His wife, Marta, was spearheading an attack on Bullard and had a new bomb-maker, plus a plant in Bullard's organization, some mercenary named Jerome."

Bullard clapped his hands. "Kudos to our inside man."

Reeni smiled. "This undercover agent's report just threw Jerome under the bus."

"Not only that," Trevor noted, "but gives the names of the terrorist group members who had settled here, including alternate addresses for them. Wow. The local cops will love this."

"Speaking of cops"—Damon looked over at Bullard—"wanna do the honors?"

Bullard nodded. "Time to get the cops over here, so they can get this information to round up the gang and also to take Jerome off our hands." Bullard pulled out his phone. "How the hell will I explain how we came into possession of this undercover statement? You think the cops will be mad that we entered their crime scene and interrupted the chain of custody with this piece of evidence?" He didn't wait for an answer, just smirked and dialed.

She gave him a hard look. "Just keep me out of it. Other than that, tell them whatever the hell you want."

Trevor smiled, picked her up, and swung her around in a huge flying hug. When she finally was on the ground again, he kissed her hard.

When he lifted his head, she smiled up at him. "I'm not sure what I did to deserve that," she muttered.

"Lots of things," he said, smiling. "You're finally coming into your own, and I love it."

She hesitated, frowned at him, and asked, "You're not scared of me?"

He chuckled. "No, not in this lifetime, absolutely not."

She smiled. "Good to know. I always worry how people view me."

"People who don't know us will probably always have something to say," he replied, "but the people who do know us will have a whole different story. You come home with us, and Terk will want to spend some time with you."

"Yeah, I don't know about that. I don't really know him, don't really know anything about him. Even though I could really use some training, he doesn't run a home for runaway psychics."

Trevor chuckled. "That has been mentioned a time or two." Just then his phone rang. He looked down at it and smiled. "It's Terk." He put it on Speaker and said, "Hey, boss."

At that, Terk laughed. "Since when do you ever call me boss?"

"We pretty well got our answers," he began, "but you should see what Reeni did." He quickly gave him an explanation.

Terk laughed. "Now that's a skill I could use. So, Reeni. … Are you coming over here to spend some time?" he asked to the room at large.

At that, she frowned and asked, "How did you know I was here?"

"Because your energy and Trevor's have been linked since the beginning," he replied. "We don't shy away from that kind of thing here."

She hesitated at first. "I would like to come, but I'm still dealing with a lot of stuff."

"That's good," he noted, "and we're all dealing with a lot of stuff too. Maybe when you're here, you'll have a chance to deal with some of that. Plus, we have healers here who can help you," he added. "Make plans to come back with Damon and Trevor." And, with that, Terk ended the call.

She looked over at Trevor. "Does Terk just expect everybody to obey?"

Trevor smiled. "He's also a precog, so, if he saw you there, he probably wouldn't have wasted too much time with explanations, just would have extended the invitation to get your ass in gear."

She smiled. "It would be nice to find acceptance," she said in a small voice. At that, a gentle arm patted her on the back. She turned to see Leia, smiling at her.

"There is acceptance here too," she shared, "particularly now."

Reeni rolled her eyes at that. "I'm really not into doing

demonstrations like that."

"In this case it's much appreciated," Leia noted. "No bloodshed, which I'm grateful for because I wouldn't want to spend the afternoon in surgery. I also won't deal with Jerome's burns. The police can do that."

"Or, you know, maybe Bullard will," Trevor noted. "I think at the moment he's trying to figure out what happened to that young man."

"Jerome took a wrong turn in life somewhere," Leia explained, "and he couldn't wait for somebody to see how majestic he is."

Reeni rolled her eyes. "Sounds like a lot of us are pretty messed up on the inside."

"But not you," Leia stated, giving her a gentle hug. "You're doing just fine."

TREVOR STUCK CLOSE to Reeni. The rest of that day and even the next were fairly traumatic for her. The police were back and forth at the compound. Statements were taken. More statements were made, and the whole time Trevor felt her nerves, afraid that somebody would mention her part in it. Sure enough, she was mentioned in the sense that she had been taken by the gunman, but something had gone wrong, and his own gun had misfired. Then somehow he had electrocuted himself.

The cops were all stunned and confused, and nobody had any idea how that worked. The police certainly didn't understand, and neither did the rest of Bullard's team. By the time the explanations were done and dusted, it was well into the afternoon of the next day.

As Reeni sat here, nursing a cup of coffee, Bullard walked in, with a big smile. "I hate to say it, but you'll have to make a trip to the US."

She winced, knew what was coming. "God, I really don't want to go to Texas, don't want to confront my father," she muttered.

"You're not going alone. My lawyer is going, and Trevor, and we might just send a team, in case you need them there," he shared.

"What are we going for?" Reeni asked.

"The judge is hearing your side of the story, and, with both your mother and your sister free, they'll be speaking as well," he explained. "They're also asking if they can see you. Apparently your mother has some apologies she wants to make."

Reeni groaned. "That sounds like heavy storm weather coming soon."

"It is, but it's heavy weather you need to bear," he stated, glaring at her.

She glared right back and snapped, "Says you."

"Yep," he agreed instantly. "I'm calling the shots, not you. So you get your ass over there and fix this."

She looked over at Trevor. "Do you think …"

He smiled cheerfully. "I'm coming with you. I won't leave you alone at this stage."

She smiled, then looked over at Damon and asked, "And you?"

"I'm heading home to my family. Then I'll see you in a couple days."

"You will?" she asked.

"Yeah, when you get to the castle."

"Castle?" She stared at him in shock.

"Yeah, that's Terk's place, and my home base," Damon stated, with a huge grin. "It's quite something," he added, with a boyish grin.

"It really is quite something." Leia chuckled.

"Now that is something to look forward to," Reeni stated, looking over at Trevor. "Why didn't you tell me he had a castle?"

"Because I wanted you to come for me," he said in a dry tone. "Not for the castle."

She felt the heat roll up her cheeks, not ready to have this personal conversation in front of everyone. "It's not as if we've had any time to discuss *us*, especially not alone."

"Nope, no time alone, but we'll fix that," he declared, with a note of humor.

"Yeah, sure, maybe after this business with my father though."

"Sounds good to me," And, with that, he looked over at Bullard. "How're we getting there?"

"My plane's taking you over." She stared at him, and he nodded. "I'm coming along too, to ensure nothing else goes wrong. I don't travel commercial if I can avoid it."

"Nice job if you can get it," she muttered.

"It sure is." He chuckled. "That flight is on the agenda for two days from now."

She paled, but Trevor pulled her closer and whispered, "It will be fine."

She took a deep breath, then nodded. "For the first time I think I might believe you."

"As you should."

CHAPTER 11

I T WAS ONE thing for Reeni to face her father. It was another thing to see her sister and her mother, when they finally met up three days later. It involved tears, hugs, tons of emotions, and lawyers who were trying to prep her for her courtroom testimony.

She just frowned at them and stated with a finality that no one could argue with, "Look. I'll tell the truth. There is no need to prep me on what to say."

When she was called to speak with the judge, she walked up and told him exactly what had happened and what she'd been through for many years. The judge kept asking questions, and her father kept trying to interrupt, but, at the end of the day, he could say absolutely nothing to convince the judge. All the documentation against Reeni had been overturned.

She stood here, releasing a long sigh of relief, as her father was warned about the court cases piling up against him for all his shenanigans, including tax evasion, fraud, and some other things she didn't know anything about. When she felt an arm around her shoulders giving her a hug, she turned to see her sister, tears in her eyes as she whispered, "Thank God, I didn't think I would ever sleep again."

Understanding exactly how her sister felt, Reeni murmured, "Now we can sleep. It's been a hellish period of too many years, but it's over."

Her mother came over and asked, "Are you leaving now? Are you going away for a long time?"

She hesitated, and Trevor walked closer. "What do you want to do, Reeni? Do you want to spend a couple more days here or head straight to the castle?"

She groaned. "I really want to go to the castle, but …"

He interrupted, "Why don't we compromise?" He looked over at the two women and smiled. "How about we stay for a couple days, and then we'll come back in a few months for a longer visit."

"That would be lovely," her mother said. "And I really owe you a lot, all of you, for getting us out of that nightmare."

"That was her doing," Bullard said, pointing at Reeni. "She's not the easiest person to work with, but she gets there eventually."

She gasped, then caught his big grin and glared at him. "You'll pay for that," she muttered.

"Yeah? I'm still paying for that," he said, with an eyeroll. "Apparently you've not seen the bill to fix my gate."

She smirked and then couldn't stand it and broke out laughing. "Yeah, but I bet you won't do it again."

"What are you talking about?" her mom asked in confusion.

Reeni smiled and gave her a gentle hug. "It's all right. Mom. It's nothing."

She spent the next few days getting to know her family again and enjoying every bit of it. When the time came to say goodbye, she was honestly choked up about it. Especially seeing her sister with her kids again.

"We'll come back," Trevor promised her, and she nodded.

As they boarded Bullard's private plane again, she asked Trevor, "So did we just shanghai Bullard's plane?"

"Well, Bullard went home, delivered everybody else, and came back for us, although he does have a couple stops along the way to make."

Shaking her head in amazement, she got on the plane to start the next leg of their journey.

By the time the journeys in the air were over, they were now driving on land, as Trevor pointed to the castle in the distance. Reeni stared at it with wonder. "My God, it really is a castle."

"It really is," he said, with a yawn, and she realized just how tired he was.

"I'm sorry," she muttered. "It's been an emotional couple days for me, but, for you, it must have been incredibly boring."

He laughed. "Not boring at all. You've blossomed so much that it's been a joy to watch."

She smiled at him. "You do say the nicest things."

"It's easy to say nice things to nice people," he replied.

"So, does that mean, as far as everybody here is concerned, we're an item?"

"Only if you want to be," he said.

"I definitely want to be an item."

He glanced at her and then pulled the rental vehicle off to the side for a moment to stare at her. "This is a hell of a time to announce that."

"It's not as if I've had time," she said, with a smile. "We've been a little busy."

"We have, and I've definitely tried to keep my distance, so I didn't cloud up your homecoming with conflicting emotions."

She shook her head. "Nothing conflicting at all," she murmured. "Just emotions."

"It'll be late when we get in," he noted. "So no getting to know anybody tonight. We have rooms to ourselves, and we can start getting to know the group tomorrow."

"And each other?"

"How much getting to know each other did you have in mind?" he asked, chuckling.

Once she realized her father would no longer be in her life, her focus on self-preservation abated to be replaced by this edginess. More and more she wanted to be here with him. "All of it," she stated. "I want it all. I want a relationship. I want permanency, and I want forever." She watched as the breath caught in the back of his throat. She nodded. "You weren't expecting that, were you?"

"Nope, but I am nothing if not adaptable."

She grinned. "That's good because you better get us someplace where we can have some alone time. I think we need it."

"We can hole up at a hotel that's not very far from here, if you want. It's located between here and the castle. We could spend a day or two there."

"That's perfect," she said, nodding. "It's perfect. We need a couple days just for ourselves."

Before long, he pulled into the hotel and signed up for the first night. As they got into the small room, she looked around and smiled. "I love it. It's so quaint." Indeed, it was. The four-poster bed came with heavy curtains hanging around it. "This is almost like a castle."

"The castle is only a few minutes from here, and we can still go there, if you rather."

"No, we need some time to ourselves first," she murmured. "Can you let Terk know?"

"We won't need to," he muttered, with a dry tone. "He already knows."

She looked at him and smiled. "Good, that saves us a lot of time on explanations."

As soon as he turned around and put his phone and car keys down, she asked him, "Unless you want to go."

"No."

"Will you be embarrassed?"

He looked at her. "Sweetheart, we'll have our own room together, the two of us, at his place. There's no embarrassment."

"Oh." Her eyes widened. "Why didn't you tell me that?"

"Because you're the one who wanted time alone, and I'm good with that too." He opened his arms, and she raced into them. "Having a little bit of time to ourselves is not a problem. When we first arrive, it won't necessarily be very private, not with getting to know everybody and what they can all do."

"I didn't even think of that," she muttered, pulling back and looking at him. "Do they all have ... *abilities?*"

"Yes." Trevor smiled. "Some of them are pretty wild."

She grinned. "I can't wait."

He lowered his head and whispered, "You'll have to for now, at least until the morning."

She felt the heat from his lips and that whole sense of relief—not only for having this whole mess over with but also having time with him. To have a whole night with him was beyond imaginable, and to think that they had a lifetime ahead of them was something she couldn't even begin to dream of.

He lifted his head and smiled. "Yes, it's time for us and whatever we want to make it."

She smiled, tears in her eyes. Then she watched as the concern drifted through his gaze. She shook her head. "They're happy tears."

"If you say so. I'm not too sure about this whole happy-tears thing."

She chuckled. "It's all good." She grabbed her T-shirt from behind her head and quickly pulled it off. She thought nothing of it and just tossed it to the ground.

His eyes widened. "It's that way, *huh*?"

"Definitely," she murmured. "I wasn't kidding when I said that we needed to find some time for ourselves," she noted. "I didn't really want to attack you the minute we walked into the castle."

He burst out into delighted laughter, even as he stripped as fast as she did. She still beat him and stood there in front of him in nothing but socks. He looked down at the socks, and a huge grin crossed his face. Shaking her head, she quickly pulled them off and tossed them to the side as well. She walked to the bed, flipped back all the covers, got in and stretched out, with her arms wide open.

"Sweetheart, you go from zero to sixty in a matter of seconds," he murmured, as he joined her in the bed.

"That's okay. I'm hoping you're a bit of a speed demon too, at least for our first time."

"Damn right," he muttered, "but then we'll have all night to go around this track, time and time again."

She gave up even trying to talk, pulling his heavy, warm, muscled body down atop hers, her thighs opening wide, as she gripped him hard around the hips. She felt her body already opening for him, something she had wanted so badly but hadn't even allowed herself to consider.

She hugged him tightly and rolled him over, and she sat atop him. His gaze went wide. She continued to watch his facial expressions, as his hands covered her breasts, and her hands held them there. She slowly lowered herself onto his erection, shuddering with joy as he filled her to the top. Just as she seated herself, he arched deep within her, lifting her completely off the bed. She cried out as her body exploded at the unexpected push.

By the time her own emotions had eased somewhat, she looked down at him and whispered, "Oh boy."

"Yeah, oh boy," he repeated. "It'll be one of those nights."

He started to move, but she told him to be still. She leaned forward and started to move. It took them seconds to sync, and then she was driving just as hard and as fast as she could, especially now that she knew what was waiting for her. Soon he collapsed beneath her, as she followed him once again into the abyss.

WHEN REENI WOKE up the next morning, her body was sore and achy but warm, held deep within Trevor's arms. His breathing was slow and steady beneath her ear. She lifted her head and looked up at him and saw that he was smiling at her.

"Hey," he greeted her, sliding down a little lower to give her a good morning kiss. "You okay?"

"A little achy," she admitted, with a cheeky grin, "but I earned it."

He chuckled. "It was a little rough at times."

"No, I wouldn't call it rough," she corrected, "but a very active night. I don't think we got much sleep." She grinned up at him. "But what we got was that time together that I desperately needed. Now my suggestion is a shower and then maybe hit the castle for breakfast. I have visions of a huge dining room table laden with food." She rubbed her tummy. "By the way, sex makes me hungry."

He groaned and then laughed as he got out of bed, picked her up in his arms, and carried her through to the bathroom, where he turned on the shower. "Sweetheart, any appetite you've got, I am more than happy to satisfy."

He placed her under the water and gave her a deep soul-searching kiss, before grabbing the shampoo. "We have all the time in the world, and no matter what time or what place," he whispered leaning into her, "I'll always be there for you." He gave her the tenderest of kisses on her nose, on her chin, and then finally on her lips, bringing tears to her eyes.

She wrapped her arms around his neck and whispered, "Thank God, because I'll never let you go."

EPILOGUE

T ERK LOOKED UP with interest as the newcomers arrived at the dining room table. He recognized their appetites and the cementing of the bond between them, and he nodded. "Welcome," he said. "Your rooms are ready whenever you want to take your luggage up."

"I don't have a whole lot," Reeni murmured. "I need to go shopping somewhere along the line."

Terk nodded. "I'm sure a bunch of women here would like to go shopping with you."

She sat down across from him and reached out for a handshake, as she smiled and said, "Thank you."

He gave her a gentle smile in return. "What are you thanking me for?" he asked, amusement rippling through his tone.

"I don't know whether it should be for giving me a place to stay or for the support I've needed or for the help with my father or for tossing Trevor in my direction," she replied. "I have a lot of reasons to be appreciative, but one of them is the acceptance of what I can do or not do, plus the willingness to give me a chance to learn some more."

"For that you are welcome," Terk replied. "I've checked out your energy, and an awful lot is going on in there. You have some stuff to get rid of, and you've got some things that need fine-tuning," he shared, "but you should be quite a sharpshooter by the time you're done."

She tilted her head to the side and frowned. "What does that mean?"

"You should be able to direct that electrical energy wherever you want it to go. And, if we gave you some jewelry, maybe some metal bracelets," he added, looking down on at her fine-boned wrists, "that might help you to direct your energy, even when your target can't conduct your electricity," he suggested contemplatively.

Her gaze narrowed as she stared at her fingers and her wrists, saying, "That sounds like fun."

He grinned. "Any games we play along that line will be most interesting because I can guarantee that nearly everybody here will want to take part in it."

She realized for the first time that there really was a profound sense of connection and community here. And she would also learn more and understand her gifts better.

THE NEXT MORNING Terk sat at his breakfast table, the gang in front of him, and smiled. "Looks like we got that one beat too," he said, with a smile.

Celia nodded. She was looking a little tired. He gently pulled a lock of hair off her cheek, and she smiled. "I'm fine. It's just the babies keeping me up."

He nodded, knowing full well what a toll the babies took on her and yet what quiet joy she took in working with them on a constant basis.

At the same moment, Damon walked in.

Terk smiled at him and said, "Sounds like a job well done."

"A job well done, indeed, but it was a bit dicey there for a while. Once you get lawyers involved, it can get pretty ugly."

Terk laughed. "Isn't that the truth. We have plenty of lawyers that we're dealing with in our way too."

"Problems?" Damon asked.

"No, not at all, just setting up all the business stuff that still needs to be done," Terk replied, waving his hand about.

"And, speaking of all that, where's Riff?" Damon asked in a curious tone. "I didn't see him on this job at all. Usually he has a habit of popping in and out, like a bad penny."

"Usually he does. He got another lead on his fiancée's murder," Terk replied. "So he's off on that again."

"One of these days," Sophia interjected, from the far end of the table, "we must have something solid to go on to help him out."

"We're still looking," Terk muttered in a dark tone. "Aren't you?"

"I am. We all are. When we're not on jobs, we all pitch in, looking to see what we can find for him. There's just … not much there."

Terk nodded. "We will find something eventually. However, with Angela back and forth, looking after babies," he added, with a laugh, "it's not like we get a chance to avoid *that* issue."

Sophia nodded. "Those two are an interesting couple. Yet they're rarely ever here at the same time."

"I'm pretty sure that's by choice," Celia shared. "You and I both know something is between them, something that's unfinished and that needs a resolution on this murder case first, before they have any chance of going forward with a healthy relationship."

"And both would tell you right off the bat," Damon

shared, with a wry smile, "that neither of them wants to move forward with anything that involves the other. ... We all know that would be a lie. At least not so much of a lie as just not acknowledging what's in front of them. Mostly I think out of loyalty to his ex-fiancée—equally for both of them."

"Isn't it great how we get ourselves all twisted up on things like that?" Lorelei pointed out, as she waddled in, with her massive belly.

Terk shook his head and said, "I presume Angela's popping in soon, with your due date approaching."

"She should be," Lorelei said, with a laugh. "Hey, that's the way it works between doctor and patient."

Terk nodded. "At least she's here when we need her, and, when we don't, we know everything's good." He looked around and noted, "Not sure we have any more jobs at the moment. I think we should all enjoy a few days' worth of a well-earned rest."

"The minute you say that," Gage declared, as he walked in and sat down, "it's almost an invitation for trouble."

"It is, indeed," Terk agreed, with a laugh.

When Jonas phoned just a few moments later, Terk sighed. "I never should have mentioned taking any days off." He answered the phone on the second ring. "What's up, Jonas?"

"The government wants to thank you for your service," he began, with an ironic tone.

Terk laughed at that. "Glad to hear it. Still, I can't imagine that's all you are calling about."

"Regardless, I'm pretty sure that this is a good partnership," he said.

"Yeah, we were just talking about the fact that we don't have a job on our list at the moment."

Jonas snorted at that. "Don't look at me. I'm trying to take some time off. Although … I did pass your name on to another department."

"Yeah? What department is that?"

"MI5," he said quietly. "Something homegrown has soured."

"Soured how?" Terk asked, raising an eyebrow and looking around at everybody.

"In this case it's jewel thieves. The last group, a team of four, went in, took everybody hostage, shot up the security guard and the store manager, grabbed everything inside the shop, and then disappeared. They've done this three times now."

"Why is MI5 interested?"

"Because it's been linked to a local terrorist group," Jonas explained. "I don't know if that's just a cover or a convenient smokescreen. However, I did tell MI5 that they may very well contact you, if they need a hand and want to get the case locked down. Of course that doesn't mean they believe me."

"Not sure I want to work for somebody who doesn't really see the value in our work either," Terk replied.

"Don't be so stuffy. If they haven't worked with you, they don't know what you can do. The head guy knows a little bit, and he knows that your track record is pretty special."

"Is there anybody local in particular working on this?"

"He's got, … jeez, who is it now? … Morrison Hadley. Yeah, his name's Morrison, and he has been tracking them for quite a while. He possibly has an inside line now on something because one of the security guards' sisters was actually on the scene at the time of the shooting, and she said she recognized one of the crew."

"So then why do they need me?" Terk asked, frowning at his team members gathered around the table. "If he's already got an inside line …"

"I think more or less because the sister said something about *This is a Terk job*. When Morrison relayed that to me, I presumed that this guy or the whole group—or team or whatever you want to call these people—I gather they have abilities."

"Well, shit," Terk grumbled. "That's not good."

"Exactly," Jonas said, "which is one of the reasons why I thought maybe you needed a heads-up." He added almost apologetically, "I know Morrison's good. I just don't know if he's *your* kind of good. I don't know if he's got any of *your kind* of gifts," he shared, with emphasis. "Yet the guard's sister was pretty adamant."

"You have a name for the sister?"

"Yeah, Sadie," he said, "Sadie Templeton."

"Good, in that case I'll be in touch with them."

And, with that, Jonas signed off.

Terk announced to the others, "This one could get ugly."

The team nodded in unison.

"But, if we've got people with abilities doing high-end jewelry robberies and shooting people," Gage noted, "you know we have to go after them."

Terk nodded. "At least we're in agreement on that."

Just then his phone lit up. He looked down and shared, "MI5 calling. You guys ready for this?"

They all nodded. "Absolutely."

"Here we go." Terk put it on Speakerphone.

This concludes Book 12 of Terk's Guardians: Trevor.

Read about Morrison: Terk's Guardians, Book 13

Terk's Guardians: Morrison
(Book #13)

Morrison had been shadowing the jewel thieves, searching for a pattern, … a motive, … something beyond mere greed. His instincts whispered of a bigger scheme lurking behind these heists, yet uncovering it was proving more elusive than he had anticipated. He was always a step behind, chasing shadows, until fate finally dealt him a card he could play.

Sadie was in the jewelry store, lost in her excitement to see all these beautifully crafted gemstones, when chaos erupted. The robbery was terrifying enough, but a chilling familiarity about one of the masked figures sent shivers down her spine. Her heart ached at the thought, but silence was not an option, especially when the stakes were this high …

Thrown together by circumstance, Morrison and Sadie form a fragile alliance, one fraught with tension and unspoken attraction. As they delve deeper, the lines between family and foe blur, and their quest to prevent another nightmare becomes as much about trust and betrayal as it is about stopping the thieves.

Find Book 13 here!

To find out more visit Dale Mayer's website.

https://geni.us/DMSMorrison

Author's Note

Thank you for reading Trevor: Terk's Guardians, Book 12! If you enjoyed the book, please take a moment and leave a short review.

Dear reader,

I love to hear from readers, and you can contact me at my website: www.dalemayer.com or at my Facebook author page. To be informed of new releases and special offers, sign up for my newsletter or follow me on BookBub. And if you are interested in joining Dale Mayer's Reader Group, here is the Facebook sign up page. http://geni.us/DaleMayerFBGroup

Cheers,
Dale Mayer

About the Author

Dale Mayer is a *USA Today* best-selling author, best known for her SEALs military romances, her Psychic Visions series, and her Lovely Lethal Garden cozy series. Her contemporary romances are raw and full of passion and emotion (Broken But … Mending, Hathaway House series). Her thrillers will keep you guessing (Kate Morgan, By Death series), and her romantic comedies will keep you giggling (*It's a Dog's Life*, a stand-alone novella; and the Broken Protocols series, starring Charming Marvin, the cat).

Dale honors the stories that come to her—and some of them are crazy, break all the rules and cross multiple genres!

To go with her fiction, she also writes nonfiction in many different fields, with books available on résumé writing, companion gardening, and the US mortgage system. All her books are available in print and ebook format.

Connect with Dale Mayer Online

Dale's Website – www.dalemayer.com
Twitter – @DaleMayer
Facebook Page – geni.us/DaleMayerFBFanPage
Facebook Group – geni.us/DaleMayerFBGroup
BookBub – geni.us/DaleMayerBookbub
Instagram – geni.us/DaleMayerInstagram
Goodreads – geni.us/DaleMayerGoodreads
Newsletter – geni.us/DaleNews